FAR FROM HOME
BOOK ONE

CITY *of* LIGHTS

Kelly Byrd

LONGBIRD
PUBLISHING

Far From Home, Book One
City of Lights

Published by
LongBird Publishing
Nashville, Tennessee

Copyright © 2020 Kelly Byrd

ISBN Number: 978-1-7366174-2-7

Library of Congress Control Number: 2021906811

Subject: JUV037000 JUVENILE FICTION / Fantasy & Magic
JUV001000 JUVENILE FICTION / Action & Adventure / General
JUV0140000 JUVENILE FICTION / Girls & Women

For Elly and Grayson.
The two little girls
(now warrior women)
who convinced me that everyone should have a chance to fly.

CITY of LIGHTS

CHAPTER ONE

Four children sat on the floor of a living room, huddled around the coffee table. Two of them were very animated, gesturing at each other and shouting about 'the rules.' They were all intent on a brightly colored board game in front of them.

"Admit it, Katie. You're cheating!" one of the players yelled. He had straight, shaggy black hair and was about fourteen. He sat up on his knees, a finger pointed mercilessly across the table.

"I am not!" the accused girl named Katie shouted back. She was younger than the boy, with thick sandy-blonde hair pulled back into a low ponytail, and a smattering of freckles across the cream-colored bridge of her nose. "I rolled a seven and I got Park Place, fair and square."

"Yeah, but you shouldn't be able to afford to buy Park Place and put six houses on it," the third player said, matter-of-factly. He sat with one brown leg folded underneath him, the other foot flat on the floor, with his chin resting on his knee. He was the kind of person that you could tell would be tall once he stood up. "You just landed on Sam's hotels last turn and said he cleared you out of money. How are you buying all of this now?"

"EXACTLY!!" the boy who had spoken first, the one named Sam, cried. "This is why we never want to play with you little kids. It's not fun…"

"*LITTLE kids*?! You're only THREE years older than us," Katie shot back. She looked from one boy to the other defiantly, as she knew three years was a lifetime. She said to the second one, "Brandon, you can't prove I was cheating. I have the extra money, deal with it!"

At that, Sam stood up from the other side of the coffee table. He tried to reach behind Katie, whose back was against the sofa, but she batted at his hands the sofa. "I am going to get some juice. Mary, you put the game away."

"But—" the girl started to say, then thought better of it, as she reached underneath the table to retrieve the game box.

"Do you know what kind of juice you have?" Katie called from across the kitchen, as she opened the cabinet doors one at a time. She could never remember where Mary and Sam's family kept the cups. Mary stacked the different colored bills into the correct piles.

"Um, I think—"

"Never mind, I found it," Katie said, and poured herself a cold glass of apple juice while Mary Jingo silently folded the game board and put it away.

Mary and Katie took their bikes for a ride up and down the neighborhood streets. Mary rode, thoughts lost in the clouds, swerving slightly back and forth. She would never understand why Katie and Sam were so mean to each other. Sam was never that rude to Mary when it was just the two of them around the house, or even when Brandon came over when Katie wasn't around. But every time Katie came around, Sam started calling them little kids and treating them like he was so much older and wiser. Mary just guessed that it must be tough to be someone's older brother.

Mary and Katie found themselves on their bikes because Hannie, Mary's mother, had come in from gardening to find them about to press play on their second superhero film of the afternoon.

"That's enough TV," Mary's mom said crisply.

"But Mom," Mary protested, about to explain that they had already tried non-television activities—the board game with Brandon and her brother earlier that day—but Mrs. Jingo would not hear it.

"It's a perfectly nice Sunday afternoon," Mrs. Jingo said and shooed them out of the house.

By 'perfectly nice afternoon,' Mrs. Jingo meant that it was hot and steamy in only the way coastal South Carolina can be right on the edge of summer. The air felt thick and hot, as if breathing were an underwater exercise. It was only May. Next week, Mary and Katie would graduate from fifth grade and be prepared to start middle school in the fall.

They glided by live oak trees and magnolias; past perfectly planted lawns that sparkled green like emeralds in the fading summer light. The came to a cul-de-sac not far from Kiki Patterson's house, one of the girls in their grade at school.

"Next year is going to be SOOOOOO different," Katie said over her shoulder. "You, me, and Sam will all be at the same school. Do you think he'll be a butthead to us there?"

"Probably," Mary said, as she stood up on her pedals to catch up with Katie. Sam had told her that the sixth-graders almost never saw the ninth-grade students, but she decided to keep that to herself. She looked towards her right, wondering if Kiki were home, when a sparkling flash caught her eye.

"Have you heard about this new app? I think it's called Wendy, or Whitney, or something," Katie called. She did not realize Mary had stopped. "Apparently Carlos Diaz downloaded it and his likes exploded overnight. He has like 40,000 followers now."

"Wanda," Mary said, feet planted on the ground, as she stared at the Patterson's house. "My dad has been helping with some research or something for it."

Mary saw it again. A giant burst of golden light, like a firework had gone off just above the bushes.

7

She dismounted from her bike and put down the kickstand. She then lost all track of time.

"BOO!" Katie yelled, right into Mary's ear. Mary jumped, as Katie cackled with laughter, her green eyes dancing. Mary looked around and realized that they stood in the middle of the Patterson's front yard. Mary's and Katie's bikes were propped on their kickstands, still in the street, some yards away. Mary had no idea how she had to come to be next to the bushes.

"That wasn't funny," Mary said, running to the street, mounting her bike again and riding away from her friend.

"Oh, come on, Mary. What did you stop for? I called your name and you didn't answer me," Katie said, as she trotted across the lawn behind Mary to her waiting bicycle. "Were you in a trance or something?"

Mary's mind whirled, as she and her friend headed back down the street, towards their respective houses. She could tell Katie what she thought she saw, but she was certain it was just a trick of the light. She decided not to answer.

"MMMmaarrrryyyyy," Katie sang in a high-pitched voice. She pulled up next to Mary.

"KKKaaattttiiiieeee," Mary sang back, as she allowed a smile to crack across her face.

"What did you say the app was called?"

"Wanda."

"Oh right. What a weird name for an app. Wanda."

"Must be nice if your mom lets you have apps… or a phone."

"Cheer up, Mary. You get a phone next year."

"Yeah, and my mom will still have ALL the passwords."

Katie looked at Mary and stuck out her lower lip. Katie took on a terrible fake British accent as they reached the turn for her street.

"Toodly-loo, Mary. See you at school tomorrow."

Mary laughed and waved at her friend as she rode off down the street. Maybe Mrs. Jingo was right. It was a perfectly nice day to be outside.

Mary had a particularly normal day at James B. Edwards Elementary School. She had woken up and put on her uniform. It consisted of a pair of knee-length khaki shorts that she hated, a navy-blue

T-shirt with the letters JBE printed in white across the front, a pair of cute, but well-worn red Converse Chuck Taylors, her signature pink headband, and a vintage Kermit the Frog wristwatch. (Mary wore her aforementioned wristwatch because first and foremost, she was not allowed to have a cell phone. And also she had a strange birthmark on the inside of her right wrist that greatly resembled a fingerprint. A fingerprint, that is, if someone had first dipped their finger in livid purple paint and then pressed down very, very hard.)

She had sat in her assigned seat, done her assigned math problems, eaten a peanut butter and jelly sandwich with a side of seaweed chips for lunch, and filled in a map of the United States with all fifty states and their capitals. She missed one state. Just one. Des Moines, Iowa always stumped her.

In ELA class, Mr. Schroeder had asked all of them to write an end-of-the-year essay outlining the three things they had enjoyed most about elementary school, the three things that they had enjoyed the least, and the three things they were looking forward to the most in middle school next year. Mary had written a longer essay than she'd intended about how she was finally allowed to have a cell phone next year, and she could not be more excited. She had also written how much she enjoyed school itself and was going to miss it over the summer.

Mr. Schroeder had put three golden stars on the essay, and returned it to her with a quiet, "Great job!" When he asked if anyone wanted to stand up and read their essay in front of the class, he had pointedly looked her direction. Mary had felt like a rock had dropped into the pit of her stomach. Secretly, she would love to share. But first, she didn't want everyone to laugh at her, and second, who wants to admit to being the kid who is going to miss school all summer? Mary had sat quietly at her desk while three other kids (Katie included) got up and read their essays with ease.

At 3:31 p.m. (thanks to her Kermit wristwatch), Mary shouldered her forest green backpack and walked through the double glass doors of the school towards the bike racks that sat in careless rows beside the carpool line. It was hot, bright, and humid again, and would only grow more so over the next three or four months. Sweat glistened on her forehead as she navigated between all of the other students (which was about half of the student body) who rode their bikes to school. It took her exactly ninety-three seconds to locate her lime green beach cruiser in all of the chaos.

Mary pulled her bike up to where her friends were standing. They discussed the state capitals test, and whether or not they would be allowed to go to the movies that weekend. One of the girls played the newest pop song from the speaker on her phone.

"Did anybody see Carlos today?" Kiki Patterson asked, trying to play it cool. It was a well-known fact that Kiki had a giant crush on Carlos. "I looked for him at lunch and didn't see him anywhere."

"I heard his family was on a wild vacation in Barbados," one of the other girls said, swiping her finger across the screen of her phone. "See."

She held up the screen to show a photo of a smiling Carlos and his two sisters on a beach with white sand.

"Weird for them to take a vacation so close to graduation," Kiki remarked, a note of disappointment in her voice. The other girl shrugged and asked what everyone was going to wear to the ceremony. Mary and her mom had already picked out a dress with flowers all over it online. It was on its way in the mail. All the other girls were talking so fast, Mary didn't have a chance to tell them this.

After a little while, Mary told her friends that she had better head home and threw her leg over her bicycle, was careful to look for traffic, and peddled off.

Mary took her usual route. She passed house after house, smelling trees and plants and some kind of new fertilizer that Mr. Morris must have been trying out. Mary had a very keen sense of smell. In fact, Mary's father, Harold Jingo, told a story of how Mary once, as an infant, had become so overwhelmed by her Aunt Hilda's perfume that she had fallen asleep for three solid days. As Mary coasted by, the houses all stared blankly back at her in a kind of unencumbered sameness.

As she came to the turn for her street, she looked both ways and turned the wrong direction, heading towards Kiki Patterson's house. The golden burst of light she had seen the day before had bothered her all day at school. She would find herself wondering about it or what could have caused it. When she got to the Patterson's front yard, she jumped off her bike and set it on its stand. She started across the grass, hoping that none of the neighbors were watching out their windows. She went to the side of the house, but didn't see anything. She even crossed to the back yard and did not realize that she had made a loop all the way around the house until she stood in the driveway, face to face with Kiki, who had just gotten home from school.

"Hey Mary," Kiki said slowly, removing her helmet to show the dark black twists of her hair. "What are you doing?"

"Oh, um, hi, Kiki," Mary said, trying to think of a reason why she would be circling the house of one of the coolest girls in school. "Katie and I were riding bikes yesterday and I, um, lost an earring and thought it might be in your yard."

"You and Katie rode your bikes into my yard."

"Well, not really, but you know how it goes…"

"I'm not sure I do," Kiki placed her hand on her hip and stared at Mary through narrowed brown eyes.

"I'm sorry, Kiki. I need to get home," Mary said, embarrassed, as she walked past Kiki, towards her bike.

"Why don't you ever talk, Mary?" Kiki said to Mary's back, as she started to wheel her own bike into her garage. "I know what it feels like when you think everyone at school thinks you're weird."

Mary didn't turn around to see Kiki's concerned smile. Mary simply put her leg over her bike and felt the sting of tears in her eyes as she headed towards home. She turned into her driveway a few minutes later and swiftly dropped her bike in front of the garage. She ran up the sidewalk, wanting to get up to her room as quickly as possible so she could think about how weird she was in peace.

"Mary!" her mom called as Mary closed the front door. "Did you actually put your bike in the garage?"

"Sam can do it later," she said.

Mary hoped for two things. One; that today would finally be the day her mother would believe that her older brother would put her bike away for her. And two; that this would finally be the day that Sam put her bike away. Which, as everyone (Mary included) who knows about brothers knows, Sam would not.

"It's not Sam's responsibility. It's yours," her mother said.

"Okay!" Mary groaned.

Mary opened the garage door and pushed her bike inside. The garage was a mess of knick-knacks and souvenirs that no one had ever gotten around to throwing away: her dad's out of use wood-working shop, an old golf-cart with miscellaneous parts that were in a heap in the corner. No one would ever park a car in the Jingo's garage. It was where all the stuff that had once been very exciting but now quite forgotten went to die. Mary pushed her bike among the random mess of things and turned to go back outside.

She snagged her wristwatch on a broken beach chair as she headed for the door. "Ow!" she exclaimed.

As she turned around, fingers around her wrist to ease the sting, she caught a faint golden explosion on the edge of her vision. Feeling the prick of Kiki's words, she already felt weird enough for one day. She shook her head and pulled the garage door closed.

As she turned to go back to the house, the golden glow caught her eye again. Mary stood in front of her garage, watching the glimmer play off the corner of her house. She lost the fight against her curiosity and followed the sparkling light around the corner. She gasped as it now floated in the air above the retention pond in the back yard.

She started towards the pond. She breathed deeply of the air but didn't smell anything out of the ordinary. Nothing past the dirt and trees and the faint but still discernible smell of chicken her mother must be making for dinner.

She came to edge of the water and as she did, the glowing circus of light stretched and shrank.

"I'm coming closer," she whispered. "Don't disappear!"

As if it heard her, the glimmer's strength reappeared and it shone brighter than ever.

"Well, I can't get to you," she said, a little louder. "I can't walk on water."

"What was that?" Mary's father said, from the open kitchen window that overlooked the back yard. Mary jumped like someone had snuck up on her.

"You scared me!" she said. She glanced at her father, and looked back at the shining spot above the pond.

"I'm sorry! I burned a cake earlier and was letting the smoke out. But I need to close this window. It must be one hundred and fifty degrees out there."

Mary nodded.

"Mary…are you okay?" Harold asked, a concerned look in his eyes. Her mother always said that Mary and Sam had inherited the Jingo eyes: small and slightly tilted, with a rich, dark brown color. "Usually you would make a joke about how bad my baking is."

"Yes…yes…," Mary said, slowly turning to face the window. "I'm fine."

"Well, okay! You should come try this cake! It is very burned and may taste like a piece of charcoal—oh wait, hang on," her father said, cocking his head to the side and listening. Mary laughed and dramatically rolled her eyes.

"Don't roll your eyes at me, young lady!" he said with a laugh. "Your mother says, 'Did you put your bike away and that your brother's home and we are going to eat.'"

"I did and I'm coming," Mary said.

"SHE DID AND SHE'S COMING!" her father yelled over his shoulder. "Okay, ta-ta for now!"

Mary turned in time to see her father pull his white-haired head back in the window and close it. Kiki was right; she was weird. Whose dad said, "Ta-ta for now" and meant it? She glanced back towards to the pond. The golden glow almost disappeared in the failing light. She must be imagining things.

Mary couldn't sleep that night. She lay in her bed tossing and turning and absolutely unable to keep her eyes closed for more than a few seconds at a time. Mary had not thought about anything besides the glimmer since that afternoon. She had been able to see it ever so slightly through the window behind her dad's head at the dinner table. Every time he would shift position for an especially dramatic part of the same story he told every night over dinner, the glimmer would be there, shining like the most imperceptible invitation the world has ever known.

She could have said something. Several times, as she moved her broccoli around her plate hoping that it looked like she was about to eat it, she thought about asking someone to go outside and investigate the situation with her. But Katie didn't see it yesterday. And her dad hadn't seemed to notice it when he had shouted her name out of the window. Mary didn't really feel like speaking up. She felt weird and uncomfortable in her own skin so much of the time as it was in the fifth grade, even when she wasn't seeing things. She was convinced that was she was going crazy or getting sick. She had no interest in being made to go to the doctor.

Mary's blankets were pulled up to her nose and she peeked around them. She made a promise to herself that if she saw any more shining, glimmering, golden balls of light floating over shrubs or ponds tomorrow, she was going to tell her mom, even if that meant a trip to the eye doctor. She took comfort in this personal deal and was just ready to roll over and try for sleep one more time when she heard a large thump come from the ceiling above her bed.

Mary lay in her bed thinking that this was either her imagination or she had finally fallen asleep and this was a dream. (Your narrator would like to note that neither of those suspicions were true, as she heard the thump again.)

She remained motionless, staring at the ceiling and counting the time between thumps. In one way, they sounded perfectly normal. It could be a lost squirrel, trying desperately to get out of the attic. But, in another way, the thumps sounded deliberate. As if someone was tossing large, heavy objects across the floor.

Mary had a choice to make. She could very easily go to her parents' room, wake them up and tell them something was thumping upstairs. She could even yell their names until one of them came to check on her.

She could wake up Sam and ask him to come listen. Or she could go investigate the noise herself; grab her flashlight and scramble up the attic ladder to see if a poor squirrel were trapped and set it free.

The thumps continued at their irregular pace—thumps that sounded like they were for her.

Something twisted in Mary's insides. She was just so tired after the last two days. Not only was her whole life changing with a transition to a new school next year, she was just days from graduation and things were WEIRD. She was weird, Kiki Patterson had confirmed it, and weird things kept happening all around her. For whatever rhyme or reason, Mary decided she had had enough, grabbed the flashlight from her bedside table (that she kept for reading after lights out and hurricanes), slipped her feet into her favorite pair of fuzzy pink slippers, and took off for the attic. Her Kermit the Frog watch, so handy at hiding her birthmark, lay forgotten. Its ticking face pointed uselessly at the wall.

She tiptoed down the hall carefully, making sure not to wake anyone. Now that she was out of her room no thumps could be heard. Maybe it had been her imagination after all. She carefully lowered the attic ladder and began climbing the rungs, trying to make sure that her flashlight didn't slip out of her hand. As Mary climbed to the top of the ladder and popped her head into the attic, she was very surprised not to shine her flashlight on a trapped animal but a little man, standing on an old rocking horse, with an ancient encyclopedia in his hand that was almost as large as he was. He jumped visibly when he saw Mary and dropped the book, making a large thumping sound.

"Hello," Mary said. She swallowed the lump of surprise in her throat. He looked so strange, his features were so irregular, that Mary did not consider for a moment the need to be afraid.

"Hello?" he said. "Hello indeed! This has taken entirely too long. Lower your flashlight girl. We've got things to do."

CHAPTER
TWO

Mary had thought he was a man, but he may not have been human at all. Even from where he stood on the rocking horse, his head barely came up to Mary's chin. He had a large head about the size of a football turned on its side with two button ears pasted to each end. He was completely bald on the very top of his pale pink-hued head. His white hair flowed out like a regal crown. The rest of his features were irregular, like they had been selected at random.

Mary must be dreaming. Yes. That was it. She was dreaming, and she'd better wake up. Now. She reached over and pinched herself, which only succeeded in making her wince in pain and her flashlight beam wobble.

"Stop that!" the little man said.

Mary obeyed him and at once stopped pinching herself. She did not turn the flashlight off, though. She wasn't about to be left in the dark with this very strange, very old… person?

He must be very old, Mary thought. *It's taking him a really long time to get down from that rocking horse.*

The little man laughed out loud. The child's thoughts were so unguarded, she had no idea she was broadcasting a Mindspan towards him like a TV with the volume turned up to 100.

"What's funny?" Mary asked.

"Nothing, nothing," the little man said. "Put that light down. I can hardly see what's in here."

"Who—" she began.

"Ah!" the little man said, cutting her off and walking in her flashlight beam across the floor.

"What—"

"No."

"How—"

"Uh-uh."

"Why—"

"Are you finished yet? Or do you need to say 'When?' and finish the whole set?"

Mary could do nothing but stare. She remained speechless.

"Well, all right then," the man said, standing just in front of her now and peering up at her through the half-illuminated darkness. "I'm not here to answer any questions. So, there's no point in asking. You're a difficult one, Mary Jingo. You see the beacons. You've seen TWO of them. But you would not follow them. And then, why, I had to drop that book for over half an hour before I even heard the slightest sound from your bedroom. To think! I thought you were going to go ask your parents or that other boy for help, and this trip would have taken even longer. I would have had to make a really drastic move then. And, the Emperor knows, even at this present time. I hate making drastic moves."

The little man sighed and rolled his eyes. Mary just stood and stared at him. Stared at his absurd array of features. Stared at his mismatched pants and shirt.

"Mary Jingo," he continued, softer now and with less impatience in his voice. "I need you to come with me. I know, that probably seems strange, especially since I haven't answered any questions. But really, honestly, I need you to take my hand. And come with me."

"My parents say to not trust strangers," she said automatically.

"Your parents sound like very wise People."

"You are a stranger."

"You sound slightly less wise."

Mary looked at him. She pursed her lips and took a step back.

"I didn't mean that. Look, Mary, I know all of your fifth-grade sensibilities are telling you I'm crazy and that your parents will kill you. Maybe that I'll kill you, which is a stupid thought. Well, not really a stupid thought; you don't know me at all and I am glad that you are trying to trust your instincts. And, this journey might involve some mortal peril, but you'll be all right. ANYWAY, I need you to come with me," he said.

He stretched his palm upwards toward her and opened his hand. A small butterfly sat on his palm. It was the strangest butterfly she'd ever seen. It shook and glimmered like the light over the pond. Mary was entranced. It was beautiful. It gently alighted from the man's small palm, glimmering and swirling and almost losing its shape and came to rest on the end of Mary's nose. As it did, her sense of smell exploded with all the good things she ever remembered. Like hot chocolate chip cookies and her mother's hair and the first flower she would pick during spring. All these smells mixed together and folded Mary into the best feeling she'd ever felt. It was light and refreshing and completely aware. She smiled at the butterfly cross-eyed as it burst into a million tiny silvery-gold sparks and slowly disappeared. As it disappeared, so did the smells. Mary was again aware of things that smelled like attic, which included moth balls and other less pleasant odors.

She looked down at the little man again who was staring at her eagerly.

"What was that?"

"That, my dear, was the Everything," he said, a gentle smile on his mismatched face. "Mary. Please. Take my hand. Come with me."

She looked at him and he looked back at her. Mary had so many questions. So, so many questions. She did read an awful lot of books and this was beginning to feel like the start of a good one. But, she guessed, this wasn't the type of journey where questions were answered as soon as you asked them.

"How can I trust you?" she said, thinking back through everything he had said. "You even said that you *could* be here to kill me."

"Oh dear," he said quietly, with a peculiar smile on his face and a slight tsk between his teeth. "That is the only question you have asked that is worth asking. Trust. Who and why and how to trust. You can see the beacons. We've been sending them for months and not one of your People has even given them a second look. But here you are, seeing and smelling and accepting the Everything without even knowing what it is. It's not me you should trust, as something much bigger has chosen you. But, you should always trust your instincts, Mary. What do your guts say when I do this?"

He made a sweeping motion with his arms and again Mary smelled it. She smelled the most wonderful things in the entire world. All the things that she could sit and smell forever. Like peppermint sticks, Christmas trees, the asphalt after a good hard rain, and her father's shaving cream. She breathed in deeply and the little man smiled.

"You have so many questions. I understand. Regrettably, I am not the keeper with the grace to answer them. Come with me."

It wasn't a time for pacing the floor or not knowing what to do. Mary had to act. And she had to know where that smell was coming from. She needed to smell it again. Even then, it was quickly fading from the air around her, leaving her feeling desolate and full of moth balls.

Mary acted. She took two large steps across the floor and gripped those five very small fingers. She missed the grin that spread across the little man's face as he said quietly, "That's a girl. Now, on to the Adventure."

CHAPTER
THREE

Now, reader, I know what you're thinking. Whatever happens next is going to be greatly mysterious and unexplainable. After all that smelling and silvery-gold goodness, you would think you would see swirling colors or at least a large flash of light.

Nothing of the sort happened.

Actually, the most spectacular event that happened was that Mary fell asleep. Or that was how it felt. One second she had grabbed the little man's hand and the next she woke. She felt a little groggy and heavy, like she did on winter mornings when her mother would come find asleep under three blankets and tell her to get up for school.

The greatly mysterious part was that when she opened her eyes, everything had changed.

Mary opened her eyes slowly, registering that she had indeed been sleeping. Maybe she had been asleep the whole time and was just waking up into another dream.

As she sat up and looked around, she saw a lot of green grass. It was the nicest smelling grass Mary had ever met. So nice in fact, Mary almost introduced herself.

The little man was gone, completely vanished. She looked around for him and thought about calling out, but whose name would she call?

Mary realized it might be impolite to sit in a field and shout, "Little man! Little man!" Which it would have been; seeing as how she had just met one of the most powerful beings in LeeChee and had only slightly sensed it. But of course, she had no way of knowing that.

Mary sat there for quite some time, wondering what to do next.

She sat atop a low hill, and looked at the green grass hills that rolled away from her in both directions. The sky sat over them, the brightest shade of blue, and heavily cake-layered with white clouds that would have made for perfect shape guessing games between she and Katie. She turned a full circle and only saw grass and hills. She finally gave up the spinning and chose a direction to start walking, now very sad that the only thing between her feet and the grass were some flimsy slippers.

She picked a good direction, because it wasn't long before she came to the top of a hill and found herself looking down on a portion of a medium-sized town, a small stream running around the ring of its border. From her hilltop view, Mary could see row upon row of small one-story brown buildings, all with matching windows facing each other, that went on past Mary's view. The lanes and streets of the village were laid out in a perfect grid pattern inside the circle of its walls. On the side of the stream closer to the hill where Mary stood, giant crop circles (Mary couldn't think of a better word for them) flanked each side of a wide, black road that snaked its way from the town up into the hills. They looked very strange from above. She studied one set. The innermost circle was cut into four quarters, two green and two black, and was surrounded by a black ring of pavement. Four small black roads through the green grass connected to a larger paved road, around which sat several buildings and sheds. Each building attached to the outermost circle by a black spoke of pavement. From the top of the hill, it looked like a giant black and green wheel on either side of the road.

The town and the circles looked very modern and boring and empty. Mary didn't see anyone else around, no activity, no cars or trucks or anyone as she headed down the road to cross a small bridge leading towards one of the main streets of the town. While she was unsure what to do, she needed someone to help her, or at least tell her where she was, so she headed towards the ghost town. She felt a little fearful, but also excited, in a complicated mix of emotions that overwhelmed her so much, she had no choice but to keep moving.

She found a path sloping down the hillside that looked like it hadn't been used in a very long time. The grass was high on either side of it, and Mary was careful where she stepped, as her fuzzy pink slippers were not the most stable option for downhill hiking. Mary followed the path until it connected to the main road leading into the little village. By the time she made it to the main road, she was exhausted. She had been walking for over an hour and her stomach rumbled. That was a bad sign that this wasn't actually a dream. She had never been hungry in a dream before. Wasn't she supposed to be in her bed asleep, not traipsing around who knows where by herself?

The main road was made of dark pavement with a line down the center that she could only imagine was meant for traffic to go both ways. Mary took off one of her slippers and gingerly put her foot down on the pavement to see if it was too hot to walk on. It was surprisingly cool. She took her other slipper off and carried them both in her left hand as she made her way towards the town she had seen from above.

As she grew nearer to the stream circling the wall of the town, she came to an intersection where she could turn either right or left towards one of large, concentric sets of grass and pavement rings she had seen from her hilltop view. They were much bigger than she had anticipated, but not as far from the town as they had seemed from the hilltop. She could take a left or right turn down the paved road and investigate one or the other of the strange crop circles. Or she could keep walking towards the gate of the city that was now clearly in the center of her vision.

The outermost ring of either circle was heavily populated with buildings, so Mary decided to take a look and see if anyone was around. She decided to take her chances with the one to her right, for no particular reason at all. She stood at the intersection of the main road and looked up. Two large poles stood on either side of the pavement with a sign strung between them that said, "Please watch for traffic as you head towards the Flight Zone." And then, as she passed under it, she turned to see on the other side, "Please watch for traffic as you head towards Greenberg." Mary walked under the sign and stopped in the intersection of the large outer circle and looked both ways. Where was everyone? Buildings ringed the paved road, their doors and windows facing in towards the road. The building closest to her had a sign above its doors that read "Crazy Mike's Flike Storage." And in smaller letters beneath "Loey Cody inspected and approved!" Mary looked around at the random collection of buildings, reading the signs.

"Imperial Guard House; The Snack Zoo: Treats for you and your Bird; Spokes and Chains," she read aloud. Where was she? None of this made any sense. She began walking again, heading towards the smaller inner paved circle that ran around the one made of grass. Across the back of one of the buildings the words "The Resistors LIVE!" were graffitied.

Finally, she came to the edge of the smaller paved circle. (The walk from the main road to the actual grass circle was not a short walk. It had all looked so much smaller from the top of the hill.) A split-rail fence ran around the entire circumference of the grass and came up to Mary's chest. The circle itself was divided in quarters by a similar split-rail fence. At the entrance to each quarter, a large gate stood open. Next to each gate was a booth with glass walls, like the one Mary had seen in a movie where People could buy tickets to ride the subway in New York City. On the outside of the booth was a dusty sign with blue letters that read, "Air Authority: Flikes." All around the fence, were signs at random stuck into the grass that said things like: "Caution—wait for clearance of incoming riders before taking flight." "Any falling/unsecured belongings will result in a fine by Imperial Officers."

Lines painted down the center of the pavement in yellow lead away from the booth so that traffic could go both ways. Mary stepped on one of the lines and it began to glow brightly under her foot, until it almost blinded her. She jumped back. As she stepped off of it, it dulled. She stretched her neck and looked around, trying to figure out what or where she was. For some reason, Mary did not feel the urge to walk onto the grass. Maybe it was all the signs stating that no unauthorized entry was allowed.

Mary turned around and headed back for the outermost rings, thinking to herself that if that is where the buildings are, then the People must be there too. After several minutes, she came to Crazy Mike's Flike shop and took another right, walking between the buildings, carefully inspecting each window and door as she went.

The buildings on either side of her were made out of a clean brown brick, and were of different heights, some only a single story, some two or three. Every window was dark or boarded over and it was deathly silent. Something told Mary that she was not alone, though, as if a hundred sets of eyes were watching her through the empty glass windowpanes. She clenched her teeth and walked a few more steps. She did not like the smell of this place. The whole town smelled like fresh paint and pine cleaner, as if it were trying to hide a much worse smell underneath. As Mary walked, she caught the scent of something else. Something prickly and skittish, like it might run away if she touched it. It put an uncomfortable knot in her stomach and made her feel squeamish all over. If she hadn't been so desperate for answers or if the smell had been any stronger, Mary would have turned heel and run away.

She kept walking, looking at the blank, smudge free windows of the houses, thinking that someone might come out and say hello. No one did. She walked past an empty grocery, a clothing store, and a salon. Their storefronts were gleaming, but the lawns were overgrown with weeds and tall grass.

At the grocery, Mary decided to try her luck with knocking on the door. (Mary was hungry, which may have been the only reason she made this decision.) She walked up the sidewalk. The prickly smell she had smelled before became stronger as she approached the building. She gently tapped on the door. No one answered. She stood for a few seconds and tapped again. This time, she heard voices and the smell intensified. It became so strong that Mary wanted to cry out for her mother, or go hide under someone's bed. The door didn't open and Mary needed to get away. She couldn't stand that smell. It was making her sick. She darted away from the door, towards the street. She couldn't help but feeling that this was the worst decision she had made in all of her young life.

Mary stood in the middle of the deserted street, unsure of what to do. She turned a few circles and considered trying another one of the shops along the way. The clothing store had looked all right, after all. Maybe someone inside would give her advice. She walked up the street towards the building, but was again stopped in her tracks by the smell. She looked around at the brown houses, down at her pajamas. She needed to leave and she knew it.

She walked back the way she had come, feeling a little more relieved with every step. Once she reached the intersection of the outermost circle and the road, Mary instantly felt better. At the border of the buildings, it was like the smell vanished. Mary walked back towards the landing zone she had investigated earlier, past one of the ticketing booths, put her back to the split-rail fence and sat down.

What had she done? Why had she trusted a stranger, even if he did look like a house elf and a goblin rolled into one? At this point, she was very hungry and very tired. If this were a dream, she would very much like to wake up soon. This was quickly turning into a nightmare.

As Mary's eyelids became heavy and drowsy, she looked up and thought that she saw a bird circling above her in the sky. It didn't matter. She would wake up in her bed soon enough anyway. A heavy feeling quickly settled over her and she drifted off to sleep.

Something pinched Mary on the side.

"Sam!" she mumbled, rolling over.

"What's a Sam?" she heard a voice say. It sounded very small and far away.

"Sam? What are you talking about?" a second voice responded. It sounded closer, but still small.

"She just said, 'Sam' when I pinched her. I'm asking you what a Sam is."

"How am I supposed to know what a Sam is?"

"Give the child some space, Bobble and Mikeala," a third voice said that sounded like it was a few steps away. "We don't want this to be too rude of an awakening."

"She's not waking up. Let me pinch her again!" the first voice exclaimed.

But Mary was slowly waking up. Her bed felt mildly uncomfortable. It had a very grassy texture to it.

"Well, you said that you knew as much as Rickface about *their* world. I'd thought you'd know at least what she's going on about," the second voice said. Mary was almost entirely awake now, but she couldn't remember where she was and thought it best not to open her eyes. Especially since three unnamed People talked so close to her face.

"I do know as much as Rickface! But this is only a child. What if this is one of ours that wandered out of Greenberg?" the first voice replied. Mary thought the voices sounded old and young, as if they'd been around forever, but had never quite changed. The first voice continued with a tone that clearly stated its pride had been wounded. "But if this CHILD is from the Shadowlands… Let's see, I think Sam is a nation or a country. Look what they've sent us, Mikeala, a crazy nationalist. Leave it to the Resistors to bring a dangerous criminal into our midst!"

"Bobble, you are a Resistor," the third voice, a female voice. It responded to Bobble with a small laugh.

"Right, Bobble," the second voice said. "Y*ou* are a nationalist and a Resistor! She's not dangerous. She's sleeping. Sleeping objects or animals are never dangerous. It is a she, isn't it? Look at these clothes, with dishes and spoons and cows and moons. That cow looks like it's jumping! Imagine, jumping cows! Sam must be a very magical kingdom. We've never once made a cow jump."

"When has it ever mattered if a person is a he or a she?" the second voice said, with that same prideful tone. "I'm sure they'll tell us when they wake up. Anyway, I have made a cow jump."

"You have not!"

"I have. You just don't remember. We were big then. The sky was bluer and the Everything was everywhere—"

Mary chose this moment to open her eyes and sit up. She encountered something she wasn't altogether prepared for.

In front of her stood two very small People. Mary might have called them children if she had seen them from the back and was not, as she was now, looking straight into their faces. They were the same size and build as the little man who had met her in the attic and gotten her into this mess. They both stood in front of her with their mouths hanging open and their eyes wide.

The one on the left, and the one that Mary assumed was the first speaker, looked to be about her father's age in the face. He wore yellow and black checkered pants and a white V-neck T-shirt. He had a straw fedora pushed back over his wide, pale forehead and thick gray hair. He did not in any way resemble his voice, which was thin and a little high pitched and did not sound the least bit old. The one on the right wore a green dress that looked like something out of one her grandmother's old photo albums. It had a high neck and buttons and came down to her knees. Purple and yellow argyle leggings covered her legs. She had a wreath of shining black hair that was tied back from her glowing face. She looked slightly younger than the man, but not much. Neither one of them wore shoes. The little man's bare feet were a little bit large for his body.

Mary felt a sense of delight rising in her. These two People were good. She knew it somehow, in her heart and with her nose. She studied their faces, which she was instantly drawn to. The man had dark eyebrows that contrasted with his gray hair and creamy skin, and a large nose that settled over a small, thin mouth. The woman, had a wide face with a broad nose and a full, pouty mouth. They both had enormous eyes that were the color of the glimmer Mary had seen the night before, almost gold and silver at the same time. She felt, in that moment, that she had known these two little People her entire life and that they had known her too. That if she asked them to sing her favorite song, they would begin instantly. Or if she asked them to start dancing, they would pick the perfect beat and step for Mary to follow along to.

They also smelled wonderful. Mary could faintly sniff out the grass, it's difference in smell from any other grass she'd ever smelled, but she could also smell these two People. They smelled like the butterfly in the attic, all memories and home. Mary did something she was always too afraid to do with anyone other than Katie or Sam. She smiled and then she laughed. She laughed so hard. She laughed until tears came out of her eyes. She laughed until she was rolling around on the grass. She couldn't stop laughing. She had actually been laughing for several minutes before she realized that they both were laughing too.

"I love a good laugh!" the little man said, finally, sitting up and rubbing the tears out of his eyes.

"Me too!" the woman said.

"Me three," Mary said, holding her aching sides and looking from one good-natured face to the other. "I'm sorry. My mother would say I was impolite."

"Impolite!" cried the woman.

"Absolutely not—" cut in the man.

"Nothing—"

"—in the whole world—"

"—makes a friend—"

"—like laughing does!" the man finished as he looked at the woman and smiled.

"Well good," Mary said, laughing again a little.

"What's your name?" the woman asked.

"My name?" Mary paused for a moment. She had forgotten that they had only just met. "My name is Mary Jingo."

"Hello, Mary Jingo. I'm Mikeala. And this is my lifelong partner in keeping. His name is Bobble."

Mary beamed into each of their faces in turn. She stuttered a little, "You can call me Mary. I don't know why I told you my last name."

Mikeala smiled back at her.

"I am so glad you're all acquainted, but we should probably go," said the third voice Mary had heard earlier. She had completely forgotten anyone else was there. Mary still sat on the ground, with Bobble and Mikeala's faces inches from her own. She looked up and past them and saw a woman standing five steps away, with her hands on her hips, staring at them.

"Hello, Mary," the woman said. She was tall and sturdily built. She looked a little older than Sam, but not too much older. She reminded Mary of the high school seniors that came to her school to help them pick out fun books at the library every spring. Her hair was shaved on the sides and stood in a long, blonde wave on the top of her head. She wore all black, with high boots and a utility belt around her waist that held a dagger, several other pockets and compartments, and what looked to be chain from a bicycle. "My name is Van Clare. Bobble, Mikeala, and I are part of the Resistors and we're here to come get you. Rickface said you would arrive somewhere around Greenberg, but we were not sure where. If you hadn't stepped on one of the dividing lines to make it light up, I'm not sure how long it would have taken us to find you."

Mary looked down at the sweet-smelling grass. This felt like school, when Mr. Schroeder would explain a passage from Greek mythology and none of the words made sense.

"We also thought you'd be older," Bobble murmured. Mikeala stamped on his foot and shushed him.

"Are you going to take me home?" Mary asked, not sure of anything else to say. She suddenly felt very small and unsure of herself. "Or help me wake up from this dream?"

"I always hate to be the bearer of bad news," Van Clare said, looking briefly at her fingernails, her eyes so blue they matched the sky. "But this isn't a dream. And we do need to get out of here. Now. This town has been under Thrall for too long and it is creeping towards us now. It's lucky that we found you. A few more minutes, and we may not have been able to wake you up."

Bobble and Mikeala nodded their heads in unison, as Van Clare looked up toward the clouds and placed the palm of her pale white hand to her forehead. Mary looked around her, back towards the buildings in a ring around them. A slight brown tint covered the buildings, as if someone had put a filter over her vision. She followed Van Clare's gaze upward and a scream caught in her throat, as a giant black dragon descended on them from the sky.

CHAPTER
FOUR

It wasn't quite a dragon. The winged figure circled them once, and stirred up such a strong wind that Mary had to raise her arm to cover her eyes. The giant creature landed soundlessly on the grass on the other side of the split-rail fence. Its eyes pierced Mary with such intensity that she wondered if she would shrink and shrink until she could hide under a rock on the ground. Its body was almost ten feet long and almost as tall. The wingspan was three times that, and its beak was huge and curved. The unusual animal stood on four legs, that ended in long sharp talons, each one a pale shade of gold.

On first glance, Mary thought it was covered in scales, but the creature was actually fitted from talon to tail in a thick black armor. Unlike any other bird she had seen, it had a long tail that whipped back and forth as the creature stood quietly in front of them.

It smelled like a rainstorm and lightning, and Mary could tell that this being was powerful beyond anyone she had ever met. The creature's eyes were so intelligent that Mary was certain it had something to say.

Bobble, Mikeala, and Van Clare led Mary over to the entrance of the fence towards the giant creature and Van Clare quietly said, "Listen, Mary. Do you have Thunderbirds in the Shadowlands?"

"What are 'the Shadowlands?'" Mary asked.

"Never mind," Van Clare said, shaking her head slightly. "Do you have creatures like these where you come from."

Mary shook her head.

"I know you are afraid, Mary Jingo," Van Clare said, turning towards Mary. She looked down at her. "I was afraid, too, the first time I met a Thunderbird. Fear isn't a bad thing. It lets you know that danger may be near. But these creatures have been allied with our People for hundreds of years. If you are kind to WindRunner, he will be kind to you. Do you understand?"

Mary nodded quickly, and wondered of all things, what had happened to her fuzzy pink slippers. She had not seen them in a while.

"Do you know how to fly?" Van Clare asked.

"Like in an airplane?" Mary answered weakly.

"Have you ever flown a Flike or with a Thunderbird before?" Van Clare tried again.

"No?" Mary said, unsure of why she asked that question, but what kind of place was this if she were expected to fly?

Van Clare looked at her for a long moment. She looked at the Thunderbird and again placed the flat of her palm against her forehead. The Thunderbird bowed his large head in greeting. They were four steps away from the giant creature, which could easily reach out a talon and grab Mary by her cow-jumping pajama top if he liked.

"Listen very carefully, Mary," Mikeala said, gesturing left and right with her hands. "Thunderbirds are very sensitive."

"You have to have good manners," Bobble added, as if to point out that earlier Mary had said that she had bad manners.

"Because if you have bad manners, WindRunner could get offended and fly away," Mikeala said.

"And we only have our own rickety tandem Flike and Van Clare's Flike, and neither one of us can carry a second or third rider," Bobble added.

"So, you have to do this right," Mikeala said, honesty glowing in her golden eyes.

"Stop it, you two. Don't scare her!" Van Clare said, crossing her arms over her chest. "WindRunner is one of my oldest friends. She will be fine."

Mary stood in front of them, six eyes staring at her face (well, eight if you counted the Thunderbird on the other side of the fence), and said nothing. She felt terrified to the pit of her stomach. Plus that prickly, awful smell from the town was coming closer. All of these People spoke very quickly and did not leave her much room to ask any questions. Mary did not know what to do. Mikeala said,

"Follow our lead, Mary."

"Right you are, Mikeala," Bobble said, as he made a sweeping bow. "Well met, Mary Jingo of the

Shadowlands. My name is Bobble, keeper of the Everything, and servant to the lands of LeeChee."

"Well met, Mary Jingo of the Shadowlands," Mikeala said before Mary could respond. "My name is Mikeala, keeper of the Everything, and servant to the lands of LeeChee. We welcome you here as our guest and promise to protect and serve you until we deliver you to the proper People."

"Whomever they may be," Bobble finished as an aside.

"Well met, Bobble and Mikeala, keepers of the Everything and servants to the land of LeeChee," Van Clare said, bowing towards the Thunderbird. "I am Van Clare Renzo, Captain of the Thunderbird Rider's Corps and servant to the lands of LeeChee. I present you to WindRunner, son of IronClaw and StormBanshee, great rider of the night sky and servant to the lands of LeeChee."

"Bow!" Mikeala said, from the corner of her mouth.

Mary jumped and bowed to the massive bird. She quietly said, "Hello!" and then immediately started to kick herself for not thinking of something better to say.

The Thunderbird shifted on its massive legs and let out a low rumbling growl. Mary felt very frightened as it growled again and realized that it was laughing.

"Hello to you, too, and well met, Mary Jingo of the Shadowlands. I am WindRunner, son of IronClaw and StormBanshee. Stand up Van Clare, I am not my father."

The great Thunderbird rumbled again, its golden eyes alight with laughter. Bobble and Mikeala began to laugh as well. The sound was muffled, Mary thought they sounded very far away. The brown color seemed to be creeping into her vision. She swayed on her feet and Van Clare placed an arm around her shoulders to steady her.

"We have to get out of here," she exclaimed, "or the Thrall will have all of us asleep within minutes."

"Whatever you say, Captain," Mikeala said with a grin. She and Bobble joined hands and the air around them started to sparkle and turn gold. Mikeala raised her right hand and snapped her fingers, and two of the strangest bicycles Mary had ever seen appeared.

"Will you carry her, WindRunner?" Van Clare asked the giant Thunderbird, stepping closer to him without any fear. It made Mary feel a little bit better. "She has never flown before."

"Aye, I will carry the warrior," WindRunner said, his black eye boring into Mary's.

I'm not a warrior, Mary thought.

How do you know? You look like one to me. A voice that sounded just like WindRunner's seemed to whisper in her ear. She shook her head once and looked up at the Thunderbird. She could have sworn that it winked.

Van Clare ran a hand through her blonde mohawk and her blue eyes darted to the strange bicycle next to the one that Bobble and Mikeala mounted and back to Mary Jingo standing next to her on the ground. The air around them was thick and brown, like it might swallow them all whole. Mary coughed and felt very sleepy.

"Mary, flying is not difficult, but you must trust WindRunner. We do not usually put a child on a Thunderbird without any training, but this is not a normal circumstance. Open your mind and for the love of the Everything—hold on!"

She then showed Mary small indentations in the armor above the Thunderbird's wings where she could wedge her feet. Van Clare hastily strapped leather straps behind each of Mary's ankles then showed her handholds just behind WindRunner's head. She handed Mary a set of golden goggles and told her to put them on. Once Mary did, she said, "This is going to make you very sore at first. You are going to recognize muscles that you did not know you have. But hold on. As the bond deepens, WindRunner will give you his strength and you will find it easier and easier to fly."

"What do you mean the bond?" Mary called to Van Clare's back, as she ran through the now thick, brown air to the bicycle on the ground. Bobble and Mikeala and their tandem bicycle had disappeared. Mary could hardly see Van Clare, as she nodded in their direction and began to turn the peddles on her bicycle. Mary heard WindRunner's voice inside of her head again.

Here we go, Mary Jingo!

And launched into the sky.

Mary was flying! Flying was awful. She clung to WindRunner as if her life depended on it. The wind was rushing past her, roaring in her ears like it had at on the Batman roller coaster at Six Flags Over Georgia last summer. And then suddenly, it stopped.

WindRunner leveled out after his very fast takeoff and Mary was able to catch her breath.

Are you all right, Mary Jingo? WindRunner's voice spoke inside her head.

How are you doing this? Mary asked, her voice breathless even inside her own head.

Doing what? the great Thunderbird asked, his wings stretched out on either side of them, LeeChee shrinking below them, and Mary's stomach in knots.

Speaking to me through my head, she responded, trying not to look down. WindRunner laughed, and the sound reverberated through Mary's brain, like a powerful bass note in a pop song.

Do you not Mindspan in the Shadowlands? That doesn't make any sense. How do you speak to each other when you fly?

We don't, Mary replied.

Fly?

Yes. Well, we do, in airplanes. And I guess superheroes like Iron Man can fly, but they're not technically real. But we don't talk to each other like this either. Inside our heads. Can you hear all of my thoughts?

I would like to know more about this man made out of iron that flies. I can only hear your thoughts if you let me, WindRunner said. Windrunner flew around, above, and through clouds. When they passed through one, it was cold and wet and Mary shivered. *If the others ever catch up, the goggles you wear and they wear will allow you to Mindspan with each other. But we mighty Thunderbirds, we need no assistance. Mindspanning is something that your People learned from us. Although, I do apologize for on the ground earlier. It is thought to be quite rude to interrupt someone's thoughts without permission. You could be entitled to a piece of my armor if you would like to press charges.*

More words that Mary did not understand. And between clinging to the Thunderbird's back and trying to have the courage to look around her at the endless blue, she did not have the energy to ask.

Mary felt like she could breathe for the first time since she had gotten to this strange place. This was wrong. She knew from science class that there is less oxygen the higher something travels in the atmosphere. But this was a magical dream land where giant talking bird-dragons lived and tiny old People who could make gold sparks fly in the air, so maybe the rules didn't apply.

Mary heard the rumbling sound of WindRunner's laughter again in her head. She was nervous it might shake her brain loose.

CITY OF LIGHTS

It's the Thrall, Mary Jingo. That's why you felt as if you were not able to breathe. We are in the open air now. The Void cannot reach us here.

Suddenly something flashed and blurred on the edge of her vision. She looked over and saw Bobble and Mikeala, wearing the same golden goggles that she wore, and astride the tandem bicycle she had seen on the ground. It was flying. Ahead of them, she could see Van Clare, pedaling her feet steadily as she rode her own sleek, dark gray flying bicycle, golden goggles pressed onto her blue eyes. What kind of world was this, where bicycles fly?

They are called Flycycles or Flikes. Do not belittle them by thinking of them as regular bicycles, WindRunner said into her head.

WindRunner, why do you keep reading my thoughts?

You are speaking so loudly outside your mind. I am sure everyone in a seventeen-mile radius can hear them.

Don't worry, Mary Jingo. We'll teach you how to not be so loud, Mikeala's voice said into her mind.

Everybody okay? Van Clare's voice asked. Mary felt like she was in a group chat where everyone could talk instead of text. *Mary Jingo, how do you feel?*

I think I'm okay. Mary replied truthfully, although her legs were beginning to ache from holding their grip on

WindRunner's wide, armored back. His wings moved at a steady rhythm, like a drumbeat in a song. *This is the strangest dream I've ever had.*

Why does she keep saying that? Bobble asked and looked over at her, not taking his hands off the handlebars. She could just make out the merry look in his golden eyes behind his goggles. *This isn't a dream, Mary Jingo.*

You are not dreaming, Mary Jingo of the Shadowlands, WindRunner said.

THEN WHY AM I HERE? Mary thought to herself. A chorus of four voices responded all at once.

Oh my, Mary Jingo. That was loud.

Why is she yelling, Mikeala? Do you know why she is yelling?

It's not a bad question, but do try to not ask so loud. We Thunderbirds can hear the slightest of thoughts.

I understand, Mary Jingo. I know all of this is confusing.

At that moment, Mary withdrew. She withdrew so far into herself, that she was not aware of the wind rushing past her face. She forgot about the blue sky around her. She felt deeply embarrassed, and scared. She swayed in her seat on WindRunner's back, she felt heavy and the air around her pricked her nose. She smelled the circular row of buildings she had seen when she first arrived here. She felt the emptiness and embarrassment deep within her bones. Mary did not feel herself begin to slide off of WindRunner's back. She did not see the others frantically circling in the air and screaming her name. She was alone with her sadness and embarrassment and uncertainty. In her confusion and pain, she sobbed within herself, as she felt the need to cry and also to go home.

In that moment, a feeling rushed towards her that was so powerful, Mary felt overwhelmed with joy that made her nauseous. She was going to be all right, it would all be okay. Mary relaxed, and lost her grip on WindRunner's back, and fell out of the sky.

CHAPTER

FIVE

The next thing Mary knew, she was being released from two long, taloned feet and laid gently on the ground. She slowly blinked her eyes, the golden goggles Van Clare had given her hanging loosely from her neck. Above her loomed a giant golden beak and a set of golden eyes. They stared at her as if she were the most curious thing in the world. WindRunner's wild, powerful smell filled the air around Mary. She felt washed in a wave of comfort.

"Can you answer a question for me, Mary Jingo?" WindRunner said gently. "Do People in your world often jettison large blasts of the Everything and then fall asleep?"

"What happened?" Mary said, rubbing her eyes. She slowly sat up, causing WindRunnner to have to take a step back. Van Clare slowly descended on her Flike, to about four feet above the ground. Bobble and Mikeala sat on their mid-air tandem Flike, not far behind. Van Clare's head darted back and forth, looking all around her. When she spotted Mary on the ground, the stood up on her Flike pedals and dove towards the ground, rolling into a somersault as she landed. She ran towards Mary, her long legs swiftly killing the distance.

"Mary Jingo! Are you okay? You gave me such a scare. Are you hurt?" Van Clare said, dropping to her knees in front of Mary and touching her arms and hands.

"She is unhurt, Van Clare," WindRunner said with authority. "She was never in danger. I would have caught her no matter the distance."

"Thank you, WindRunner," Van Clare said, not looking at the Thunderbird. "I was not so worried about the fall, but more worried about that amount of the Everything being channeled or controlled by one person. Do you feel okay?"

"We used to be able to use the Everything that way," Bobble called. He and Mikeala floated one foot above the ground. Bobble stood on the rear seat of the Flike. "When we were bigger!"

Mikeala swung her leg over the front seat of the tandem Flike and lowered herself the rest of the way to the ground. Mary felt uncomfortable with their full attention on her. Van Clare looked deeply concerned, Bobble looked interested and disinterested at the same time, Mikeala looked at Mary as if she were the most special thing in the entire world, and WindRunner cocked his head from side to side, as if weighing Mary's options.

"I feel okay," she finally replied. "I am very hungry. I am sorry if I hurt any of you, although I'm not sure what I did."

"We're fine, Mary Jingo. We're worried about you," Van Clare said.

"We're not totally fine," Bobble replied, running a small hand over his wide forehead. "The Flikes are completely disabled."

Mary looked around. They sat at edge of a giant forest, the green grass thinning as it reached the arms of the trees. Giant rock outcroppings jutted out of the grass around them, and Van Clare wondered aloud if they could find one to shelter under. The trees of the nearby forest were so dense that Mary could not see through them. Looming above the trees, Mary could just make out the edge of something mountainous, as if she caught whatever it was at the right angle, she may be able to see it. Judging by all of the other experiences she had had in this world so far it did not surprise her. How far had they flown? In this world, she may well never know. What she did know, was that the sky was beginning to darken and night was coming on quickly.

"Can, we um, talk? I need some answers about what is going on and, um, what just happened to me?" As she said those words, she briefly smelled all of her favorite things, like she had in the attic all those hours ago.

"Yes! Mary Jingo! Yes!" Mikeala exclaimed. "Let's answer questions! I think it is time."

"Yes. We can answer your questions. But first, I guess we're going to have to set up camp," Van Clare said, looking around. "I don't like how close we are to the forest or the Disappearing Mountains. We've had reports that the Shoeboxians are all over the mountains. But this will have to do."

Van Clare and WindRunner set off to find a place to camp. WindRunner glided a few feet above the ground, as Van Clare strode behind him. Mikeala whirled her deep brown hands in the air, snapped her fingers and produced a slightly soggy mayonnaise and turkey sandwich, which Mary ate because she was too hungry to care.

Bobble stomped around in front of the Flikes and muttered to himself. Van Clare's Flike was gray with a slim, thin frame and spikes on the spokes of her tires. The tandem Flycycle that Bobble and Mikeala rode looked like it had been cobbled together from roughly fifteen different bicycles (or Flycycles) of all different colors, shapes and sizes. Even the two seats did not match. Above the back tire on each Flike was a small, rectangular box, that Bobble poked and prodded and even shot some golden sparks towards from the tips of his fingers.

"Nothing!" he exclaimed finally, throwing his hat on the ground and stomping on it. "I don't know whether to be frustrated or proud, Mary Jingo. I have underestimated you. I apologize."

And with that, he picked up his hat and gave her a sweeping bow.

"What do you mean?" Mary Jingo said. Mikeala snapped her fingers again and put an apple into Mary's hand. Mikeala had been steadily making snacks appear for the last fifteen minutes as they waited for WindRunner and Van Clare to come back. Mary's favorite had been a bag of crispy arare, a Hawaiian snack that her mother always kept in the house.

Bobble leapt up to the handlebars of the tandem Flike and fiddled with the gears by his feet.

"The Everything came to you and you both channeled and controlled it at the same time, even though it seems like you did not know what you were doing exactly. Do you use the Everything in the Shadowlands?"

Mary bit her lower lip and hesitated. She mustered up her courage and said, "I'm sorry, Bobble, but I don't know what any of those words mean."

She waited for them to laugh at her, or to tell her that she should know better, but they didn't. Mikeala gasped softly and said, "Oh, Mary. We have been the most foolish of foolish keepers to ever walk the grass of LeeChee. Of course you don't know any of the words we're saying! You're not from here. How could you understand? And you already asked if you could ask questions, and we've been so distracted, we didn't even give you a chance."

"Quite right, Mikeala," Bobble replied. He jumped lightly down from the handlebars of the Flike, landed on his bare feet in the grass and straightened his T-shirt. "What would you like to know?"

Now was Mary's chance. She could ask them anything, but she wasn't sure where to begin. The last few hours had been a whirlwind of confusion and mystery. If she asked herself truthfully, she would even say that it had been a lot of fun. Mary was not good at asking questions out loud, though. Standing in front of another person and asking a question could end in a lot of unknown ways. But as Mary looked at Bobble and Mikeala and they looked back at her, she had the same feeling she'd had when she first met them—like she had known them her whole life. The two ancient beings were not going to laugh at her or lead her astray. Mary looked around for a moment and asked the first question she could think of.

"What is that?" Mary said, pointing at the tandem Flycycle that Bobble was now leaning against. How it supported his weight without falling over, Mary didn't know. "I know you said before that it was a, um, flycycle? And obviously they fly. But what is it?"

"A Flycycle is a flying bicycle. This little box right here is the key," Bobble said, tapping the small black box attached to the back wheel. "This one is a little old, designed about twenty-five years ago before Cody really perfected the process, but it works fine."

"It uses the Everything," Mikeala added, when the look on Mary's face told them that Bobble's answer hadn't made much sense. "It channels the Everything into a positive energy that lifts us up, up, up into the sky."

"Okay," Mary said slowly. She eyed the Flike suspiciously. It looked so out of balance, that if she had not seen it in the air before, she would not have been sure it would make it off the ground. "What is the Everything? I heard you say before that I, I channeled it? What is it?"

Bobble and Mikeala looked at each other for a moment.

"We're back!" Van Clare called, from a few yards to their right. "We found an outcropping that we can make a little campsite under for the night. Mary Jingo, jump on WindRunner and we'll follow on the Flikes. Let's go."

Mary found herself again climbing on the back of the large Thunderbird and preparing for takeoff.

WindRunner kept close to the ground, only gliding a few feet above the rocky outcroppings and grass. He set down about ten minutes later, next to a large outcropping of stone that made a cave large enough for Mary to walk inside. He and Mary had both been quiet on their short flight. WindRunner could sense that Mary needed a few quiet moments to process her thoughts alone. A few minutes later, Van Clare, Bobble, and Mikeala rode through the grass on their Flikes, which were much more like bicycles when they didn't fly.

Van Clare dismounted and pushed her Flike into the mouth of the outcropping. She removed a small black tube from her belt and pointed it at the Flike. Mary gasped as it disappeared. Van Clare then twisted the tube with her fingers and pointed it at the floor again. With a small pop and a burst of golden light, a black leather pack appeared on the cave floor. Mary stared at her wide eyed.

"Pretty nifty, right?" Van Clare said, waving the tube through the air. "Bonnie Judde and the Father have been developing these for a couple of decades. They call it a dissipator. It uses the Everything to store a certain amount of stuff. Truthfully, I don't know how it works. Although, with the way the Everything is now, they can be a little spotty."

"Like a pocket dimension," Mary said, thinking of all of the cartoon characters who would have a weapon one second then make it disappear the next.

Van Clare smiled, as she rolled a blanket out on the cave floor.

"Sure, I guess."

"We don't need a fancy gadget to do that," Mikeala said. She snapped her fingers and the tandem Flike disappeared. She snapped again and a picnic of the strangest fruits and vegetables appeared on the blanket in front of her. She snapped again, and a small fire roared to life at the front of the cave. Another snap, two golden orbs of light flew to the corners of the cave, giving everything a dim glittery glow.

"Show off," Van Clare said with a laugh.

It was almost fully dark outside the mouth of the cave. Van Clare walked out to where WindRunner sat on the ground, his short legs tucked underneath his armored body. He was too big to fit inside the cave.

She spoke to him for a moment. He nodded, his large beak almost scraping the ground. Then he shook out his wings and launched into the sky.

"WindRunner is going to go get help," Van Clare said, walking back into the cave towards the blanket. She plopped down next to the fruits, veggies, and breads. "Nice spread, Mikeala!"

"Why can't he just take us?" Mary asked.

"Well, this is the thing you will learn about Thunderbirds," Van Clare said, pulling apart a piece of fruit that was lime green on the outside and a livid pink in the center. "They are very strong and very proud. WindRunner could try to carry all four of us. And we may make it to Luminos. But it would be a long and difficult flight that could injure him for several months or even years. I would rather not ask him to take the risk. Because if I ask, he will not refuse. Better for him to bring us help. We're only a day's flight from Luminos, so we will wait for him here and hope no one shows up while we wait. Starberry, Mary Jingo?"

Van Clare held out a piece of the pink fruit to Mary. She took it and tasted a small bite. It was sweet and tender and delicious.

"Wait—these aren't like the snacks you gave me before," Mary said to Mikeala, picking up a blue vegetable that looked like an eggplant and smelled like a pickle. "The ones you gave me before were, well, like home."

"The Everything knew what you wanted," Mikeala shrugged. "That sandwich you summoned was horrific."

Mary thought about the lumpy mayonnaise and turkey sandwich Mikeala had offered her. It wasn't like anything her mother ever made, or sent in her lunches to school. *Katie,* Mary thought. Katie always brought terrible, soggy sandwiches to school and always begged Mary to trade her part of her PB&J or some of her rice and dumplings at the lunch table. Mary always did, because what were best friends for? Her heart ached. She wished Katie were here. Katie would love this. Katie would know what to do. She hung her head for a moment and looked down to realize that Mikeala was grasping her hand.

"Okay," Bobble said, his hat and then face appearing in the mouth of the cave. "I set the wards. I hope WindRunner will recognize them when he comes back, or he may not be able to find us again."

"I set a marker one hundred yards to the south," Van Clare said. "I'll set them along the way. He'll recognize them if he gets lost."

Bobble laid down on the edge of the blanket and let his hat drop over his eyes. "I am tired."

"You're a keeper of the Everything, Bobble. You don't need to sleep," Mikeala giggled.

"An old soul can still be tired, Mikeala," he sighed, a laugh escaping from somewhere underneath his hat. It reminded Mary so much of her dad, she felt a sudden ache for home. Her eyes welled up with tears.

"Oh, Mary," Van Clare said. "What did we say?"

"I know," Mikeala said, placing her hand over her heart and the buttons of her dress. "We never answered your very important question from earlier. We can answer now if you like."

Mary only nodded, wiping her eyes.

"You asked about the Everything," Mikeala said, drawing herself up until she sat on her knees. Van Clare watched her, while still picking apart a starberry with her teeth. Bobble lay in the same spot on the ground, with his hat over his eyes.

"You asked what the Everything is. It's hard to explain. Once, I heard Rickface say that in the

Shadowlands, they call it magic. But then he described magic and it sounded wrong. The Everything is, well, everything. It is the life force of LeeChee. It makes things grow, prosper, learn, and change. It used to be everywhere, and the People of LeeChee lived in the open air, interacting and growing and changing with the Everything."

"Until...," Bobble said from under his hat.

"Until a keeper that used to be our friend turned on us. She started going into towns with her evil thugs, the Shoeboxians, and scaring People. She convinced them that it was safer to stay in their houses. We tried to stop her. We've been trying to stop her, but the more the People of LeeChee fear, the more they refuse to leave their homes, the more the Everything shrinks, the more we shrink as well."

"The town," Mary said, slowly putting the pieces together. "What did you call it? Greenberg? The one where you found me. Was that town one of the ones that, is uh, too scared?"

"Yes," Bobble said with a giggle. "They are very scared in Greenberg."

"Thrall," Mary said quietly to herself, repeating the word that WindRunner had said earlier.

"Yes, Mary! How did you know that?" Van Clare asked.

"WindRunner said something about it," Mary answered.

"You are very good at putting things together," Van Clare said, a look of admiration in her eyes. "Greenberg was one of the first to fall under Thrall, and it's been one of the last places that we haven't been able to recover."

"So, the Thrall, it's caused by that creeping brown mist that put me to sleep—"

"Yes! The Void!" Mikeala finished for her. "Isn't it awful?"

It definitely didn't smell very good, Mary was sure of that.

"We are a group of People," Van Clare added, "made of flikers, Thunderbird riders, keepers, and Thunderbirds that is trying to turn the tide of the Void. But we are failing miserably. Every day, the Shoeboxians seem to grow in strength."

"But out here, in the meadows," Mikeala said, her golden eyes gleaming as bright as the orbs in the corners of the cave. The brightness seemed to increase as she finished her sentence. "Where we can run and play— the Everything is strong."

"What is the Void? What are Shoeboxians?" Mary asked, a warm feeling settling in her stomach when Mikeala talked about the Everything.

"The Void is like the Everything turned inside out," Bobble said, sitting up on his elbows and pushing his hat back on his gray hair. "It's dark and evil and it consumes where the Everything grows."

"And the Shoeboxians are a violent race of People that live high in the mountains on the southern border of LeeChee," Van Clare said, Mary seeing fear in her eyes for the first time since she met the Thunderbird Captain. "They have always been happy to be left alone, until Mellie went and asked them to join her. They are not necessarily evil, but they are hungry. They live for the Void and love its energy. They are feeding on it, we think, and that is why they are getting stronger."

Mary had heard this story before. She had read enough books, seen enough movies, to know how the story went. What she didn't understand why she was here. She had always seen herself as more of a Steve Trevor than a Diana Prince, or a Luna instead of a Harry. She was always happy to help but wasn't meant to be the center of the action.

"So, what am I doing here?" she asked, the question that had been weighing on her since she had woken up in those hills.

"We don't exactly know," Mikeala said. "We have tried anything we could think of to turn the tide of this war. Loey Cody has a theory that this is connected to the Shadowlands. Your world and our world are connected in a way that we don't really understand. We began sending beacons to the Shadowlands to attract a great warrior to help us."

"The beacons. The little man I met. The one that was in my attic and sent me here. He said I was the first person who had paid attention to the beacons in months."

"Do you mean Rickface?" Bobble laughed. "He's a keeper like us! Yes—Rickface has not been too pleased with being in the Shadowlands for several months. He says that it stinks down there."

"Rickface," Mary murmured to herself. She filed the name away for later, in case she met the strange little man again.

"Regardless," Van Clare said, giving Bobble a good-natured shove on the shoulder. "You saw them. You responded to them."

"What does that mean?" Mary asked, twisting her hands in her lap and wondering where her headband was. How was she supposed to fight monsters without it?

"It means that you are here, Mary Jingo," Mikeala said with a small smile.

"Because you chose to be. And that is a powerful thing," Bobble finished.

CHAPTER
SIX

The sun rose brightly the next morning, shooting green sparks off the grass. The light played games with itself, rolling and tumbling around the campsite in the forms of animals and birds. Bobble and Mikeala jumped up, squealing gleefully to chase the sprinting forms, as pure dawn was one of the few times when the Everything was still able to be clearly seen.

Mary Jingo lay wrapped in a blanket that Van Clare had pulled out of her backpack, in that thin space between sleep and waking. She had laid awake for a few hours the night before, listening to Van Clare's breathing and Mikeala's and Bobble's occasional giggles as they kept watch from the mouth of the cave. She tried to fit the pieces together like a puzzle of everything she had learned so far about this strange place. That a connection exists between her world and this one. She had been chosen by some mysterious force, or she had chosen this mysterious force (that sounded a lot like THE Force, if she were honest) to come help the People of this world. The Everything was shrinking because People wouldn't leave their houses. The Everything sounded vaguely like Mary's mom, who constantly complained that everyone spent too much time on their phones, or in front of their screens. Mary's dad would then agree and head down the hall to his study to do research on the internet about ecommerce.

Mary accepted now that this was not a dream, but that did not mean that she was up to the task in front of her. She could think of seven to twelve of her classmates who were braver or better suited to this task than she was. She had pushed up her pajama sleeve and rubbed her thumb over the purple spot on her wrist. She wondered how she had ended up here, of all places. Someone like her—so ordinary. She had fallen asleep then, her brain overwhelmed by all of it and had whispered to herself that maybe this time she would wake up in her own bed. So, maybe she was still not wholly convinced about the dream thing.

"Mary Jingo?" Van Clare said gently, touching Mary lightly on the shoulder. "You need to get up. We need to move to another camp before nightfall."

Mary rolled over and yawned. Van Clare moved back over to her pack and shoved the blanket she had used inside. Mary rubbed her eyes. Light streamed in the mouth of the cave, brilliant and bright. Mary rolled out of her blanket burrito and stood up. She was aware that she needed to brush her teeth. And possibly shower. Her pajama pants were filthy around the ankles. She looked over at Van Clare.

"Do you guys use toothbrushes here?" she asked, unsure of what the response would be.

"What's a toothbrush?" Van Clare asked, standing up and holding out her hand. Mary realized that she should give Van Clare the blanket.

"Um, it's something that you use to clean your teeth?"

"Oh—a dental swab. I think I have an extra one. Hang on."

Van Clare dug around in the pockets of the pack and eventually produced a piece of fabric attached to a lacquered wooden handle. It didn't have bristles, but it did look mostly like a toothbrush. Van Clare said, "It's brand new, I promise. Thunderbird Captains always carry a spare in case someone forgets. Mikeala also summoned some clothes for you, I'm not sure from where. You'll find a stream about 200 yards that way where you can clean up. Bobble and Mikeala are outside, they'll show you."

"Thank you," Mary said slowly, holding the dental swab up in the air like it were a candle. Van Clare chuckled and went back to shoving Mary's blanket into her pack. Mary wandered towards the mouth of the cave.

"You're welcome," Van Clare called after her.

They had spent the night under a stone that jutted out of a wide, flat field that was covered at random by some of the most beautiful flowers Mary had ever seen. They swayed in the wind, their colors playing against the blue sky. Bobble and Mikeala had broken into a game of tag that Mary very much wanted to join but could tell instantly that she would lose. Every time one or the other would get far enough away, there would be a small pop and the other would appear at his or her side. They would tag each other, break into a fit of giggles and start all over again.

She wandered away from the rock, listening to Bobble's and Mikeala's laughter. She reached her hand out and touched a particularly brilliant purple flower. By its smell and the way that it looked, Mary knew that the flower was incredibly shy.

"I'm sorry," she said out loud reflexively. The flower's petals seemed to shrink a little and then they shook merrily, as if to say, 'Nice to meet you!' Mary laughed as Bobble and Mikeala ran up, and Mikeala darted behind her legs.

"You can't see me!" she shrieked. They both smelled wonderful. Like they were the morning, all bottled up and contained in two People. All the beauty and vitality in any world seemed to radiate from them.

"I can see you, Mikeala. Mary cannot make you invisible," Bobble said, swatting at Mikeala around Mary's legs.

"Yet!" Mikeala cried. With a pop she was off again. Mary wanted to know where the stream was that Van Clare had mentioned and she also needed to relieve herself.

"Mikeala!" Mary called after her, trying to catch the keeper's attention but found it difficult in the middle of the game. Mary ran down the hill after them, "MIKEALA!"

Mary tripped on a stone, her bare toes crunching on the rock as she flipped head over heels down the hill. Mary felt herself rolling and tumbling across the earth, the ground coming up quickly over and over again. On the next roll, Mary saw a giant rock. She was headed straight towards it. Mary squeezed her eyes shut and braced herself for impact.

Suddenly, she stopped.

"Mary Jingo!" Mikeala called. A pop sounded by Mary's left elbow, and Mary looked down at Mikeala's concerned face. "Are you okay? Lucky the fleurs caught you. That might have been awful. I would have never forgiven myself."

Mary looked around her. She was being held aloft by a bed of purple flowers like the one she had just met a few minutes ago.

"Thank you," she said to the flowers. "Thank you for catching me."

A rustling sound like the wind blew through the petals, as if the flowers said, "You're welcome!"

They shifted and lifted her until Mary found herself standing in front of Mikeala. Mary turned towards the flowers and brushed her hand ever so lightly over their petals. In her heart, she thanked them deeply. The flowers seemed to bow their purple heads in response.

"This is our fault, Mary Jingo," Bobble said, picking his way gingerly down the hill in a series of hops. "We shouldn't have ignored you for our game."

"It's okay," Mary said, as she straightened her pajama top and brushed off her legs as the flowers watched. She felt a close kinship to them now. She turned towards the keepers, "Do you know where I can find some clean clothes and a stream?"

"We thought you'd never ask!" Mikeala said, as she turned to lead the way. She stopped for a moment and snapped her fingers. A bowl of Mary's favorite instant ramen appeared. Mary accepted it without question.

The stream was cold and refreshing. Bobble and Mikeala wandered a little ways off to give her some privacy as Mary tried her best to remember that one girl scout meeting she had gone to with Katie where they explained how and where to use the bathroom outside. Once she had used the dental swab, and felt reasonably clean, she pulled on the clothes that

Mikeala had given her. She wore a pair of soft, black joggers and a white T-shirt that said, "LIVE FREE!" in a rainbow of colors across the front, along with a black bomber jacket with gold accents. Mikeala had also summoned her a pair of sneakers that were turquoise and yellow with matching turquoise socks, which Mary was grateful for, as she did not know how she would walk all day with bare feet the way the keepers did. All of the clothes fit perfectly and were wilder than anything Mary ever wore at home. Her mom was a big fan of practical clothes, but not so much of colors. After she dressed, she called for Bobble and Mikeala. They bounded over the hill and across the flat grass towards the stream. Bobble said she looked refreshed and as Mikeala said, "Oh! I forgot."

She snapped her fingers and produced a yellow headband. "I think you need this."

Mary smiled and accepted the headband, pushing it into her thick black hair. She felt the most like herself that she had since she had arrived in LeeChee. Mikeala said that she liked Mary's look, snapped her fingers and her own clothes changed. She now wore a pair of blue pants and a bold orange

T-shirt that said "Flikes Rule!" on the front. Her coarse black hair also became two thick braids.

"Wow! You look great," Mary said with a smile. "And thank you for the headband"

"Well, let's go y'all. We have a lot of ground to cover," Van Clare said, coming across to the stream. Her white-gold hair gleamed in the sunlight. She still wore the same all black gear she had worn the day before, but she looked refreshed in the morning light. Her black pack was slung across her back like a quiver of arrows.

"We could just stay here, Van Clare," Mikeala said. "This place is just so lovely."

Bobble laughed, as if to agree with her. Mikeala looked as she might go chasing after him.

"A sitting bird is a dead bird," Van Clare said. "We'll be too exposed after a full day of sitting. You can bet that Mellie is not sitting still."

Bobble and Mikeala consented and the four of them started off on the grass. They were making their way around the edge of the forest. Mary looked around at the grass and rock outcroppings, to the menacing trees to her right. Van Clare walked fast, with Mikeala in front of them and Bobble behind. Mary did her best to keep up. She looked up to the horizon above the trees and she could again make out the edge of something fuzzy.

Mary squinted her eyes. She didn't see anything at first, and then, as if a veil lifted, she could make out the edges of pale green mountains. They shimmered in the light as if they were on the edge of Mary's vision. When she turned back to look at them, they shimmered and all but disappeared. Their outlines still faintly shone against the blue sky.

"Mountains," she said, quietly. "Are mountains over there? I can see them, sort of. Only when I don't look straight at them. When I look straight at them, they disappear."

Bobble and Mikeala began to dance around at that, chanting to each other:

We are the mountains of LeeChee.

Now you see us, now you don't!

You might find a way over us,

Unless you are friend to the Void, you won't.

We change and hide

Not from friends, but from foes.

Will we help you?

Only the Everything knows.

"That explains a lot," Mary said, a little sarcastically, when Bobble and Mikeala had finished the first round through the song. "So, am I a friend or a foe?"

"Well, you perceive them," Van Clare said, as she stopped for moment to look around. "But you cannot see them. So, the mountains have not decided."

"Yes, well, that's all pretty and nice," Bobble said, looking towards the mountains and the sky. "But we can't navigate the forest at night. We need WindRunner to show up. Now."

"We'll rest soon," Van Clare said, shielding her eyes with her hand. "We may have to go into the forest. I don't like the way it feels out here. Let's keep moving."

As soon as Van Clare said that, Mary understood what she meant. The air felt a little icy, and Mary was happy to have her new bomber jacket. They stopped for a rest and a snack. Bobble and Mikeala seemed to be on edge. They hiked for a few more hours, the ground around them becoming less grass and more rocks as they went. They camped for the night under a similar stone outcropping as the night before. Mary had a hard time falling asleep. Van Clare did too. Mary could hear her tossing in her blanket burrito.

They started walking again early the next morning. Mary's legs were sore and tired and she didn't really want to go on. After their first morning break, Mary had a hard time finding the energy to get up and keep going.

"Are you okay, Mary Jingo?" Van Clare asked.

"I think so. My legs are still sore from flying," Mary said, standing up from the ground. "I don't usually hike like this for days on end. I'm just a little tired."

"I know. I'm tired too," Van Clare said. Mary looked up at her face and could see that the Thunderbird Captain felt the same way she did. "I thought WindRunner would be back by now, but he is not close enough to Mindspan. I am trying to stay positive."

"How long have you been a Thunderbird Captain?" Mary asked.

"Four months," Van Clare said. "I thought this would be an easy mission. I'm one of the youngest ever, made a Captain at seventeen. But, of course, it's all turned into a mess."

Van Clare ran a hand through her mohawk, which had become more of a sheet of hair hanging over one side of her head. The golden light danced off her long, slim nose and the sharp angles of her face.

"You're seventeen?" Mary exclaimed. "You're only a few years older than my brother!"

"Is that a bad thing?" Van Clare said with a wide crooked smile that did not hide the fear in her eyes. "It probably is. I can't believe I messed this up so badly. I let the Flikes get disabled. This is the worst place for us to be. I can't have the person I was supposed to rescue be captured on my first mission!"

"It's okay, Van Clare," Mikeala said, taking the girl's hand into her own. "It's not your fault the Flikes were disabled."

"No," Mary said quietly. "It was mine."

Bobble looked at Mikeala who looked up at Van Clare. They all three looked at Mary with concern and respect.

"We had no idea that you would be able to channel or control," Bobble said to Mary. She realized in that moment that he had changed into a new T-shirt at some point in the last day and a half. "It's actually quite wonderful. But sometimes, to discover a wonderful thing, you have to break something first."

Mary did not know what that meant, so she looked at Van Clare who looked very unsure of what to do. Van Clare then took a deep breath and said, "No, you're right. I may only be seventeen, but I've been training for this my whole life. Let's head into the forest and go as far as we can before nightfall."

"I don't think that is a very wise plan," Mikeala offered, looking up at Van Clare with sincerity.

"Why not? If we keep skirting the forest, we're walking away from Luminos. We're just wasting time," Van Clare countered.

"Yes, but you know how the forest is," Bobble said, taking his hat off and then placing it back on his head. "It's alive, Van Clare. It will interfere with our ability to channel or control."

"I mean, isn't it worth the risk?" Van Clare asked. "Plus, I don't like being out here in the open. It feels unsafe."

"We can only hope that the trees accept us," Mikeala said, looking off towards the forest. "They can be powerful allies, but also formidable foes."

"How will WindRunner find us?" Bobble asked. "The trees might choose to move the markers. We could be lost for days."

"The markers will work," Van Clare said. "WindRunner is one of the smartest People I know. He'll find us."

The keepers said nothing and stood side by side. They stared at Van Clare with such intensity, that Mary felt even more shy than usual, which was saying something.

"Well, I say we go in," Van Clare said, looking at the forest, straightening the strap of her pack across her chest. "And I'm leading this mission."

She took off towards the forest without giving Bobble and Mikeala a second look. The other three followed the Thunderbird Captain slowly, as if believing she might turn around and change her mind. They walked a little farther and found a path in between the trees. Mary had found the forest menacing from the outside, but once they were underneath its branches, she liked it very much. So much was alive in the forest, breathing, moving around them. It felt welcoming, like the trees wanted them to come and stay awhile.

"This is lucky," Mikeala said aloud.

"What?" Van Clare asked, stepping between roots and scrubby plants.

"The trees are happy we're here," Bobble said.

"Should we thank them?" Mary asked. She did not quite understand this overwhelming feeling

LeeChee gave her, that every blade of grass or tree or rock deserved a show of gratitude for existing. But they did.

"That's a grand idea, Mary!" Bobble said, as he walked over to a tree and laid his palm against it. "Thank you, tree."

"Thank you, tree," Mikeala said, putting her own palm against another trunk and laughing.

This significantly slowed down their progress, but the anxiety they had all felt before entering the forest slowly seemed to go away as they continued on.

They followed the path for several hours until night began to fall. They found a small clearing and Van Clare declared that this was where they would camp for the night.

Bobble and Mikeala set about drawing property lines again, while Van Clare and Mary unpacked their blankets. Mikeala said that they would not make a fire that night, as fire would upset the trees. Mary had begun to feel afraid in a nameless way, and she didn't think it were the trees that caused her unease. Night fell in inky blackness around them, and their small circle of the forest was illuminated only by one of Mikeala's glowing orbs of light.

Bobble and Mikeala sat side-by-side at the edge of the property lines they had drawn, very invested in an argument. Bobble said that a Whiffer was a pretty useless animal unless you could train it to hunt for water in the desert. Which is not an easy feat. Mikeala argued back, saying that he had it all wrong. A Whiffer was the most valuable creature anywhere because it could find fruits and berries in a twenty-mile radius. Bobble was thinking of a Snuffler. Which was useless unless you could teach it to hunt for water in the desert.

"Van Clare," Mary said slowly, knowing the keepers were too far off to hear. "Can I ask you a question?"

"Sure!" Van Clare said, eating a starberry from the cold dinner Mikeala had summoned for them.

"Do children always become soldiers in LeeChee?" Mary asked honestly. Van Clare snorted a little and choked on her starberry. Mary felt embarrassed. This is generally what happened when she asked questions. "Sorry. I didn't mean to be rude."

"No, no, Mary Jingo. I am sorry!" Van Clare said, becoming serious. "I laughed because, I am not a soldier. I'm a Thunderbird rider and Captain. My job is to help People, to serve them. It's only been in the last year that Thunderbird riders have had to fight anything. Your question makes sense, I just wasn't ready for it."

"Sorry, you just seem really young to have such a big job," Mary said. "My brother's friends work at ice cream shops and sports stores. They don't captain Thunderbirds. And most of them are still in school."

"I think I see your point, although I'm not sure what ice cream is," Van Clare said. She looked off into the dark distance, as she explained. "I actually just finished school. I may have been a Thunderbird rider since I was eleven and passed the Test, but that doesn't mean I finished scribing, reading, or equating earlier than everybody else."

"The Test?" Mary asked, pulling her piece of bread apart with her fingers.

"Yeah, the Test. You know—where they test your abilities to see if you show an affinity for the Everything? Of if you show the ability to fly, you might take up Fliking or try to ride with the Thunderbirds. Or if you're into questions, you might use the method of guess and test, you can do that too, and make new discoveries. There are more abilities that People test for—I can name them all, but the list is long…"

"We don't do that in my world."

"Oh, really? Everyone is tested here at age eleven, then you do your ability training and normal school at the same time until you're seventeen. Well, I should say if you want to. Some People choose not to be tested, which is okay too."

Mary nodded her head and took a small bite of a piece of bread. They fell into a comfortable silence. Imagine being tested this year to see if she could use the Everything or ride a Flike. It seemed she had already done a couple of the things Van Clare listed. Did any of it count?

"How it is in the Shadowlands?" Van Clare ventured.

Mary paused, trying to think of how to answer out of her own experience "Everyone goes to school until they're eighteen, at least. Well, a lot of People do. After that, you can kind of choose your own adventure, I guess. Or that's what my dad always says."

"Do People often go on adventures in the Shadowlands?"

"Oh! No," Mary giggled. "I guess I don't mean actual adventures. I mean you can choose what you want to do. You can go to college, or you can get a job, or you can go travel, or you can do none of it, or you can do something else."

"All of that sounds like an adventure to me. We have college here! It's in Luminos, where my I'm from. It's where all the great scholars live. You'll probably stay there too, since you can channel and control."

"That would be nice. We have lots of different colleges in the Shadowlands." Mary slowly trailed off then, she didn't usually talk this much to anyone but Sam or her parents or Katie. It felt odd to say so much to Van Clare at once. Van Clare smiled in the dim light. "My mom always says that I should start planning now. That I should know what I want to be when I'm older. And I don't know, it's just a lot. I'm only eleven."

"I understand. Some People say that we test too young, that children should not be hemmed in to one thing," Van Clare said, her face darkening. "But it is different in Luminos because oftentimes People learn different skills later, after they finish their first round of training. But the Test is not popular across the entire land."

"Did you always want to fly Thunderbirds?"

"Not really," Van Clare said. Mary could see her tense in the Everything orb's glow. "My dads are both great controllers of the Everything. I think they always expected me to be just like them."

"You can channel and control?" Mary said, excitement in her voice. Maybe Van Clare could teach her how to do what she had done earlier again.

"No," Van Clare said. She looked both sad and angry, as if the world were sitting on her shoulders. "I didn't pass the Test. I couldn't even accept a Mindspan from a Thunderbird without goggles or something else. So, here am I, six years later, no knowledge of the Everything. My dads say that they don't mind, but I know it's disappointing. Disappointing to have a daughter like me."

Mary looked over at Van Clare. The Thunderbird Captain looked so sad, that Mary felt like she might need a hug. Mary started to say something when Van Clare put out her hand.

"Shhh—be quiet Mary," Van Clare said, looking around. "Do you hear that?"

Above them, a bright spot of light shot out of the darkness. Mary and Van Clare watched it arc over their heads, Van Clare rushed forward and grabbed the two keepers by their collars just as a ball of fire hit the ground and exploded.

CHAPTER SEVEN

The ground around them was burning. Mary could smell the trees, their sticky scent of anger and wrath palpable at the flames.

"I knew it!" Van Clare shouted. "They've been on us all day. I could practically hear them over that last hill today. Bobble and Mikeala, you must keep Mary safe—whatever happens. If you have to run, run. You'll be safer in the mountains than here."

Bobble and Mikeala looked the closest to terrified Mary had ever seen them. Their smell was clouded too, as if a veil had dropped between Mary and her senses.

"Not the mountains," Mikeala said.

"We can help. We can," Bobble said, at the same time.

"I know," Van Clare said, her face gentle, her eyes still bright. "But Mary is more important. If this gets ugly, head for the mountains. WindRunner will find you there."

"But, what about you?" Mikeala asked.

"I will fight," Van Clare said, pulling the bike chain from the belt at her waist.

Mikeala nodded reluctantly. Bobble grasped her hand.

"Now, I need your help," Van Clare added. "We have to make a stand."

"Incoming!" Bobble yelled, pointing at the sky. Mary could see a new ball of flame arching below the trees, catching low limbs on fire. She ducked behind the keepers, as Van Clare stepped aside and it burst on the ground.

"Come on, come on!" Van Clare shouted. "Show yourselves!"

Van Clare radiated a smell of confidence. She held her Flike chain in her right hand, her left on the pouch at her waist.

Bobble and Mikeala stood to the right of her, holding hands. They were rocking back and forth and beginning to glow. Mary watched them in the light of the tiny fires as they began to grow brighter and brighter and she relaxed into the smell. That wonderful smell of all the things she loved in the world. Mikeala began singing and a jet of light shot out from their clasped hands. It began to spread and glow and form a bubble around their party. The fires inside the barrier vanished. Mary looked around at the golden dome. Shimmering particles fell from its roof.

Shapes began to appear out of the darkness, coming into the glowing light of their golden dome. At first, Mary thought a group of very short men were approaching. The sound of heavy feet accompanied the shadowy figures. As they got closer, Mary could see that the creatures looked a little like men, but weren't. They were all short and very square. Their heads were not separated from their bodies by a neck, but were a lump with eyes and a mouth coming out from between their shoulder blades. Their skin was a pale green that looked scaly and strong. Their arms and legs were muscled and terrifying. They each carried a heavy black club that looked like it could do more damage than any knife or sword—especially in those arms.

Their smell, even through the haze of goodness, was overpowering. They smelled like an animal that should have died a long time ago but had found a way to survive—a smell that barely limped along and matched the absence of light in any of the creature's eyes. They also smelled like the town Mary had stumbled across before Van Clare and Bobble and Mikeala found her. Something dark and dank that made her want to hide.

"Shoeboxians," Bobble growled. "I knew the forest was a bad idea."

He slapped his palm to his chest and bared his teeth. A golden ball of light formed in his open palm, as he still clasped hands with Mikeala, maintaining their golden half-sphere.

Van Clare took a step forward and raised the Flike chain above her head and swung in circles very quickly.

Through the shimmering barrier, small black balls went flying from the chain and hit the Shoeboxians square in the chest. Each one exploded with force and the creature would fall and not move anymore. The attacking force growled collectively and began firing back. Swinging their own kind of chains and sending red balls of light at the barrier. As each one exploded against the shimmering surface, Bobble winced a little and Mikeala made a small cry.

"Hold, Bobble! Come on!"

Van Clare was deadly accurate and the Shoeboxians continued to fall. It didn't seem to make much of a difference, Mary thought. Too many Shoeboxians advanced towards them. Not one of them even flinched as another fell beside it.

Mary could tell that Bobble and Mikeala were fading. Mikeala's will lessened and the shield was beginning to show holes along the back and sides. Bobble dropped Mikeala's hand and called the golden substance towards himself. He sent jets of silvery golden light at packs of Shoeboxians who didn't fall; they disintegrated with yelps of pain. The shield was almost completely dissolved, with only Mikeala to maintain it, and the Shoeboxians began to close in. A black and red ball of light dropped towards Bobble and hit him squarely in the chest. He fell to the ground. Mikeala screamed and grabbed at his body, the shield disappeared around them. Mikeala dragged Bobble towards Mary screaming, "RUN."

Van Clare cut through the Shoeboxians, a golden staff now in her hands. Where it had come from, Mary did not know. Even though the Shoeboxians lay in piles around them, the fight wasn't over, as more streamed out of the trees. Van Clare turned to look at Mary and the keepers, the desperation clear in her eyes. Suddenly, the Shoeboxians stopped. The stood in a ring around the four of them, but they did not continue to fight or come closer.

"Give up, Van Clare," a woman's high-pitched voice said out of the darkness. "Give up and I won't hurt them too badly."

Van Clare winced and the effort she made to stand up straighter was visible.

"Don't play with me, Mellie."

"Play? I don't play. You of all People know that. You know, Van Clare, it was brave of you to come on this mission. And to bring these two with you," the woman's voice said with disgust. Mary peered into the darkness, squinting her eyes, as if that would make Mellie appear faster. Mary couldn't help but like the sound of her voice. It was reassuring. In fact, Mary wasn't quite sure what Mellie was saying, she just knew that her voice sounded nice. She suddenly felt numb to her situation, except for the smell that crept in on the edge of her senses. It was a bad smell. She didn't like it, but the sound of Mellie's voice helped her ignore it. "You look smaller than usual, Bobble and Mikeala, which just makes me feel so warm and fuzzy on the inside. And a guest! Well, Van Clare, you said you were going to introduce me to your new friend? You're still going to make me wait? I always thought you were a coward, but this is magnificent!"

Mellie had every intention of continuing to talk, but Van Clare said, "Stop the charade, Mellie. And come into the light. Show yourself. If you're going to kill me, it's not going to be while you hide in the dark."

A long pause hung in the air. Without the sound Mellie's voice, Mary fully perceived her smell. It was bad, like Mary had thought before. But now, without her voice masking it, it was much stronger and also much more confusing. It made her feel bad, like she was just getting over a head cold, or one of her friends had told a particularly creepy story. She moved a little closer to Mikeala for extra protection.

"I'm not hiding," Mellie said, her voice made Mary's numbness return. "And who says I'm going to kill you? You know we don't kill. You can't harness the fear of a dead person. That's your problem, Van Clare. You're always putting words in other People's mouths. You're much too useful to die."

Van Clare looked too tired to respond. Her shoulders sagged slightly. Mary looked down at Bobble, who was just waking up, but still not coherent. Mikeala knelt beside Bobble, her hand on his chest, coaxing him to the waking world. Mary felt so powerless, and so alone. But these People had protected her so far. She had to do something to protect them.

"Come out, Mellie. You coward," Mary said, clenching her fists and hearing the tremble in her voice.

Another long silence reverberated. Then something rustled in the darkness. Mellie. Mary could smell her.

She shuddered as Mellie stepped into the ring of the tiny fires burning on the ground. Mary shuddered. Mellie's persona did not match her hypnotic voice. She was a very thin, very short woman with a pinched face that resembled a rat. Her small eyes were completely black with no white in them at all. They glowed black in the firelight. She had long, chestnut-colored hair that framed the pale skin of her face that was covered with a thousand tiny pink scars. She was dressed from head to toe in black clothing, much like Van Clare's, and black gloves. She looked very proud and seemed very angry.

She was accompanied by five of the biggest and ugliest Shoeboxians Mary had seen yet. Each one of them carried a much larger and much more brutal looking chain. They snarled and grinned at Van Clare, Mary, and the keepers. When Mellie spoke again, her voice had lost some of its power, but none of its anger.

"Van Clare, or is it Captain Van Clare? I always forget these days. Kathryn seems so ready just to accept anyone," she waved her hand as if waving Van Clare away. She turned to Mary, "As much as it breaks my heart, little girl, YOU should think before you speak, because you are even more unimportant than your nasty Thunderbird Captain here. Speaking up, well, it just makes you so much more likely to die. I mean, really, little girl. Did you even consider that you are completely unprotected? Look at Van Clare, she can't even channel or control," Mellie's lip curled up into a nasty smile. "But, enough talking—I'm bored. Take Van Clare and the keepers, the other one—I don't really care what you do with her."

The Shoeboxians smiled even more nastily. Mary began to panic. The closer the Shoeboxians came, the more she could smell them, the more she wanted to run. She looked at Mikeala and whispered, "Do something!"

Mikeala looked at her in bewilderment.

"What do you want me to do? This isn't the old days. I'm nonexistent without Bobble, and look at him—he can barely sit up. Besides, he has aftereffects! He can't stop giggling."

It was true, Bobble was being wrenched by wave after wave of silent giggles. He lay on the ground moving silently and twitching. It was a wonder he wasn't laughing out loud.

"I sealed his mouth," Mikeala said, as if she'd read Mary's thoughts. "It's not a particularly nice action, but he's not right. And Mellie will not be laughed at. Besides, Bobble's so stubborn; if he were right he'd have broken the seal by now."

Mary looked down into Mikeala's large golden eyes and they looked trapped. Mary felt, deep inside herself, that this was wrong. If anyone should never feel trapped, it was Mikeala. Mary had never hated anything in her life. She hated that Mikeala felt trapped.

"Mikeala, what happened to you?" Mary asked. Mary looked around wildly. There had to be something they could do. She had channeled or controlled or whatever on WindRunner's back. Could she do it again? She searched inside herself and did not feel anything but fear. She suddenly remembered the trees, how alive they were. That this was their home. She knelt down and put her hand to forest floor. Quietly she whispered, "Please. Please. Help us."

Mary looked up to see Mikeala speaking to her when time slowed down. Mikeala's mouth moved, but it took several seconds for her jaw to open. Mary turned her head, which took a lifetime, only to see the Shoeboxians unable to advance. Van Clare was frozen in mid-fling of a bomb from her Flike chain, toward one of the enormous Shoeboxian's chest. Mary looked up above her to see a massive tree limb swinging through the air. The trees around them had responded to her call. And they were angry. While Mary and her friends and all of the surrounding Shoeboxians were frozen and unmoving, the limbs above them swung quick and angry through the night air, knocking Shoeboxians clear across the forest.

The air around her snapped and time went back to its normal pace so suddenly that Mary felt it physically. Somewhere from her right, the wind from a swinging branch blew so powerfully that it knocked Mary and everyone else off their feet. A scream that sounded like Mellie's voice was heard out of the darkness. Another blinding wind blew past and for a moment, Mary could not see. She heard a Shoeboxian somewhere nearby snarl and felt another rushing wind fly above her head. Then, silence.

CHAPTER
EIGHT

Mary lay on the ground with her arms over her head, her face pressed against the hard earth. As she opened her eyes, the light around her was golden, like it had been the last two nights when Mikeala made golden orbs in the caves. Mary glanced up and sure enough, an orb hung several feet above her head. Purple flowers grew across the forest floor, stopping in a perfect ring around their party. The Shoeboxians and Mellie were nowhere to be found.

A voice that Mary had never heard before, but decided she very much liked said, "Well, here's to a big successful rescue. Not that you needed my help, hey Van Clare? You can all get up now. It seems the forest decided the battle was over and ended it for you."

Mary looked up from the ground and could just barely make out a very thin man of medium height standing within the ring of flowers, his black Thunderbird garb offset by a wild, tie-dye bandana holding back his coarse, dark afro. Mary brushed herself off and stood up. Behind him were about half a dozen very angry Thunderbirds and riders, their golden goggles glinting in the glow of several suspended orbs of light like the one above Mary now. They all hovered about a foot above the purple flowers on the forest floor.

Mary reached out and gently brushed her fingertips along one of the flower's petals. "Thank you," she said. "You saved us." The flower bobbed its petals as if to laugh and say, "We won!"

"This was one of the crazier things I've ever seen," the man said, holding out a hand to help haul Van Clare up to a standing position. "When we flew over, the trees were swinging their limbs so wildly that I watched a Shoeboxian fly ten feet into the air."

"We've got a problem," she heard Van Clare say, as Mikeala stood up too. Bobble's aftereffects had not worn off. He now lay motionless on the ground with his eyes closed.

"Problems already, Van Clare? I just told you the trees fought for you and you're all business. Besides, you took on Mellie and the Shoeboxians. Not to mention the wild gamble of going into a forest that you were not sure would be kind to you. What else could be wrong?"

"Speaking of which, thank you very much," he said first to the trees and then to the flowers, his golden brown eyes merry as he bowed ever so slightly. "You have saved a most important member of my crew."

"Is everyone all right?" Mary heard a familiar voice boom, as a rustle of wings and four sets of golden claws landed on the ground next to the man.

"WINDRUNNER!" Mary yelped and ran across the small circle of exposed ground to the giant Thunderbird. The space was becoming more cramped by the minute, as no one dared to step on the flowers. Without thinking, Mary threw her arms around WindRunner's neck and squeezed.

"Who is this kid?" the man said. "She just hugged a Thunderbird. And he let her."

"This is Mary Jingo, Commander. Mary, this is Commander Loey Cody," Van Clare said, looking tired and worn from the battle. Burn marks marred her clothes in several places. The clothing on her right side was wet. She was bleeding. "Bobble over-Channeled the Everything. We need to get him to Luminos now. He needs an oracle."

Loey Cody looked down at the motionless Bobble, concern filling his face. He went to one knee beside the keeper and placed a hand on Bobble's chest.

"You're right. Time is very short," he snapped back to his feet, concern and grief in his face. "Can you fly, Captain? You look hurt."

"It hurts. But I am okay. I can fly."

Cody stepped to the side and pulled a dissipator from his belt. He pointed it at the ground and with a pop a black Flycycle with a step-down frame appeared next to Van Clare.

"I hope the seat is right for you, we don't have time to make adjustments."

"I'll be fine," Van Clare said, shouldering her pack, which was very singed and smoking ever so slightly.

"Mikeala, take Bobble and ask BlueClear if she'll carry you. I can Flike with Van Clare," Mikeala nodded. She had said nothing since Cody and his force had arrived. She looked sick with worry and also sick herself, as Bobble's illness seeped into her. She crossed the bare ground out of earshot to a Thunderbird and dropped into a low curtsy of greeting. The Thunderbird bowed in response and consented to the passengers.

"You're with me, Mary Jingo," WindRunner said. Mary had not realized that she still held a hand to the side of his neck. The trees above them shook. Mary knew that they wanted them to leave. They had done enough damage for one night.

"We should go," Mary said without thinking. "The trees want us to leave."

"You speak to the trees?" Cody said, cocking an eyebrow at her. He was older than Van Clare, but younger than her parents. His face was incredibly pointy at the chin and as he talked, his full lips pulled into a snarl more than a smile. His black skin offset his golden-brown eyes to the point that they almost glowed. He leaned down and began to roll up his right pantleg, which Sam explained to her once that

People did in order not to harm their bike chain. "You, Mary Jingo, are full of surprises."

He stood up and pulled out the dissipator again, and made another Flike appear. This one was very different from Van Clare's. It was a heavy-duty mountain bike with thickly treaded tires and a spring below the seat. It was brightest orange Mary had ever seen and had a larger Everything box than Van Clare's did. Mary stared at the Flike. Van Clare walked over to her and put a set of goggles into her hand.

"You should try to sleep on WindRunner's back if you can. It will be dawn soon," Van Clare said. Mary took the goggles soundlessly from her hand. WindRunner nudged her gently with his beak and she walked around his wing to climb on his back. Once she was securely in the foot restraints, the great Thunderbird launched into the sky.

How did you find us? Mary asked WindRunner across the Mindspan. The night air was cold around them, and grew colder as they flew higher to crest the mountains.

We followed the markers, WindRunner said. *And then, at some point, they stopped. We would have been completely lost if Mellie had not set the forest on fire. We were able to follow the smoke right to you.*

I'm glad you showed up, Mary said truthfully.

Why? WindRunner asked. *You called to the Forest and it answered you. You did not need our help in the slightest.*

How did you—? Mary stuttered.

We Thunderbirds are different from you humans. We have not lost touch with the heart of LeeChee like you have. While we are People, just like you, a part of us is still wild, still animal. We heard your call, just as the trees and the flowers did.

Mary fell silent again. Too much had happened in the last few days for her mind to even begin to process. All the fear and anger and wonder and frustration welled in her like lava beneath a volcano.

It's okay if you explode a little bit, Mary, WindRunner said. *These days have been a lot for you, I am sure.*

Mary didn't even have the strength to answer the great Thunderbird. She simply hoped that if she fell asleep now, he would catch her. She knew in her spirit that he would. He had done it before.

As Mary drifted off to sleep, Van Clare and Cody discussed the battle from their Flikes via whispered Mindspan, so none of the other riders or Thunderbirds could hear.

Mellie is too strong, Van Clare said. *Bobble and Mikeala's shield barely stood a chance against the Shoeboxians.*

No, Cody said firmly. *I won't believe that. It had to be the trees.*

I guess the forest made a difference. Mikeala and Bobble warned me—warned me that their powers wouldn't be the same in the forest.

Don't ever do this again, Van Clare, Cody said seriously, looking towards her as the wind rushed past their tires. *You cannot just take off on missions without permission. I don't care who you take with you. The Father and Dill have been sick with worry for days.*

They're fine, Van Clare said, rolling her eyes at the mention of her dads. She hoped Cody couldn't see it behind her goggles. She shielded her thoughts from him as she made a comment to herself that she was surprised they noticed.

They are not fine. You have made all of us very proud. I don't want to have to take away your Captain position so soon after awarding it to you.

Van Clare said nothing in response. She rode her Flike in silence, the wound in her side throbbing painfully. He had no idea what the other riders said about her. That she was born to her position, she had not earned it. Even now, speaking with her dads' best friend, whom she had known since infancy, she knew that it would not be this informal if she were someone else. She needed to prove to them that she was good enough for this. She didn't need their help. She could do it on her own.

Who is the kid? Cody asked.

She's from the Shadowlands.

What?! Cody shouted, his Flycycle wobbling a little. *Holy… By the 'Cycles! She's the one? The one that Rickface went to get? How did you even find her?*

I am a Thunderbird Captain. I was in the intelligence briefing. Rickface said the hills around Greenberg, so that's where I went to look.

Well, I'm glad you found her, but you should have waited. We have already sent a stronger force to find her. I guess I'll recall them now. I said this already, but don't do this again, Van Clare. I can't have the other Thunderbird riders thinking they can just take off whenever they choose. Especially not now. You saw what happened tonight.

Yes, it happened to me and not to you, Van Clare thought, shielding her thoughts again from Cody. Van Clare again rolled her eyes. She was in dangerous territory. Friend of her dads or not, Cody was still her commanding officer. He could take her Flike away forever if he so chose.

I'm going to check on Mary, with your permission, sir, Van Clare said, looking over towards Cody through the clouds. She felt the Mindspan connection end as he placed the palm of one hand to his forehead. She pulled her handlebars and pumped the pedals until she saw WindRunner slightly below where she flew. She turned her Flike to be level with his wingtip and took up flying next to her oldest and newest friend.

Mary Jingo woke up in the most beautiful room she had ever seen in her life. For the first three minutes of wakefulness, she lay on her back and stared at the gauzy canopy over her bed. She also desperately tried to remember where she was. A brief mirage of hazy images flashed through her brain. Then, her memory triggered, she caught the rotten smell of Shoeboxian and sat up straight. She looked around, searching for an evil, neck-less Shoeboxian head, but all she saw was a circular room made entirely of windows on one side. The sun glared so brightly through the glass that Mary could only squint her eyes and look around. All the furniture in the room was white. The curtains were white. The bed sheets were white. Even the night gown Mary had on was white. The entire room was glaring.

She ventured from the bed to the curved windows. She was very high up, which LeeChee was starting to make her feel accostomed to, but she still felt a small drop in her stomach from being at such a great height. Below her stretched a massive ringed City for as far as her eyes could see. Wherever she was, she was in the center of all it. The City teemed with People, bicycles, and life. In certain areas, Flikes and Thunderbirds swooped over the walls of each ring. Some flew not too far from the window she stood behind. The City was divided into rings, each one surrounded by a giant golden wall that reflected the sunlight so strongly that the City glowed even in the bright light of day. Beyond the outermost wall, the mountains loomed, looking clearer and more defined than they had two days before. As her eyes fluttered against the light, a door in the floor sprang open. Mary turned around to find two girls about her age standing in front of the bed. One of them held an incredibly delicious tray of breakfast.

"Mary Jingo!" the one without the breakfast tray exclaimed. She was pale and rosy at the cheeks, her round face framed by a massive amount of tightly curled brown hair. "You are awake! I told you she'd be awake."

"Put the tray down, Teeny," the other said. "Mary Jingo, I'm Corb and this is Teeny. We just wanted to stop in and make sure you were okay."

They both stood close to the bed, looking unsure of what to do next. In addition to Teeny's hair, she had a large nose and small hazel eyes. She was smaller than Corb and stout. Corb was willowy and tall with long, straight brown hair that swept almost to her waist and large brown eyes that upturned at the corners.

Corb wore a green smock dress that came to the top of her golden-brown knees. It was slashed from the right shoulder to the hip with a swath of sky-blue fabric. Teeny wore a similar color scheme, including the slash of sky-blue fabric, but in the form of pants paired with a close-fitting shirt. They both wore belts with daggers and heavy leather sandals. Corb had a gold bracelet around her wrist, which Mary could faintly smell from across the room. Corb and Teeny smelled mildly like Van Clare, that peppery power smell, but it was fainter and less potent. Another smell came through as well. A smell unique to each of them that Mary knew she would be able to identify them by.

"Hello?" she said, quietly, stepping away from the window and standing across from them, also not sure what to do next. "It's very nice to meet you."

"Oh goodness!" Teeny said, suddenly, a smile spreading across her pale face and rosy cheeks. It was so bright that it broke all the tension in the air with a laugh. "We brought you food, Mary Jingo. We should eat."

Mary welcomed the suggestion and followed Teeny to the table. Corb stood in the middle of the room.

"Mary Jingo," she said, turning in a small circle, with her arms outstretched. "What's your favorite flower?"

"I don't know," Mary said, staring at the plates of bread and fruit. "I think honey suckles are nice."

"Wonderful," Corb answered and began humming under her breath. The room began to change. Mary caught a whiff of honeysuckle as they began to grow down the walls, and the furnishings changed to deep yellows, greens, and browns in order to fit the scheme. Mary's bedspread was suddenly peppered with honeysuckle flowers all over the fabric. Mary had forgotten all about the bread and watched in disbelief. When Corb finished, the room looked like a different place. She put her arms down, walked to the table and sat down next to Teeny. "There. I hate when these rooms are just white. It's so impersonal. Sorry that took so long. I'm still getting the hang of channeling."

Mary didn't say a word.

"It looks aaaa—beautiful," Teeny said, her elbows on the table, as she surveyed the room. "Do you feel tired?"

"No, not really," Corb said shaking out her hands and turning the bracelet on her wrist. Mary admired the room, looked back at the food and wondered for the umpteenth time what she was doing here.

"It's so funny, Mary Jingo. That is just what we came up here to figure out," Teeny said, spreading butter on toast, her curls bouncing in the sunlight.

"Not again," Mary said aloud. "You can hear thoughts too?"

"Oh, can I ever. You can imagine, before the Test, I thought I was going *crazy*. But evidently this is all part of being able to Control. I try to respect the Mindspan guidelines, but so many People just shout their thoughts all over the place, it's hard not to listen.

"The Father is going to *kill* me," Teeny giggled, her palm in front of her mouth. She drew herself up and put her shoulders back, and effected a deeper voice. "You listen here, O.I.T. Teeny. You must respect the boundaries. Respect the Everything. It is a privilege to use its gifts."

Teeny broke into a fit of giggles. Corb looked at her disapprovingly, but then stifled a laugh. Mary smiled to herself.

"What's an O.I.T.?" she ventured, biting into a starberry and suddenly realizing why Van Clare liked them so much.

"Oracle in Training," Teeny explained. "You haven't met the Father yet, but oh boy—you will."

The Father. That name rang a bell somewhere in Mary's mind. She couldn't place it.

"You mentioned the Test," Mary said, looking down at her hands and thinking back to her conversation with Van Clare the night before. Or had it been the night before that? Mary had no idea how long she'd been asleep. "How old are you? If you don't mind me asking."

"Not at all," Teeny said with a smile. "I'm fourteen, and Corb is thirteen. We're both into our training now. That is what the blue is for."

Teeny pointed at the blue slash across her shirt. It must have been clear on Mary's face that she didn't understand. Corb answered.

"Blue is for oracles. Black is for fliers. Green is for growers. Yellow is equators and those who do guess and test—um, there's more. There are far too many to list right now."

"It's so if you sneak out of sessions, they know who to send you back to," Teeny said with a wink.

Mary smiled. It felt like a bathroom pass that you wore on your clothes.

"So, you can Mindspan with anyone?" Mary asked.

"Technically yes, I can," Teeny said, selecting a piece of fruit from the almost empty tray. "But most People have so many guards in place, they know if you're even passing by the outer edge of their mind. And it very rude to Mindspan with someone without their permission. I really do try."

"You don't try that hard," Corb said with a laugh. Something about the way these two Oracles in Training interacted instantly took Mary back to the forest. How long had she been asleep? Where was Van Clare? Where was Mikeala?

"Bobble!" she cried out loud. "Is he okay? He was badly hurt in the forest."

The forest, the Shoeboxian attack, all of it had been her fault. Mary felt the room spinning around her. Where were her friends? Were they okay? She looked down at her plate and felt someone grasp her hand. Corb held Mary's hand from across the table. Teeny's eyes were closed, as if she received a message.

"Bobble is fine," she reported. "He was injured, but you all brought him back in time. He is healing in a room two floors down from here. Mikeala is with him."

Teeny paused. She listened to more of the message then continued.

"Van Clare is out at the Thunderbird Circles. And she would like to see you, as would Lady

Kathryn, Loey Cody, and the Father, whenever you are ready."

Mary's mouth formed the word 'how,' to ask how Teeny knew all of this information, but she stopped. She was surrounded by so much magic, or the Everything, she should learn to accept it. They had just talked about Mindspans after all, so Teeny must be sending messages back and forth with someone who had information.

"I would like to see them," Mary said quietly, still looking down at her plate.

"Yes," Corb said, a sympathetic smile on her face. She had not let go of Mary's hand. "Let's get you ready for a very big day!"

"I don't know if I can handle another big day," Mary said, letting Corb's words set in. Her face fell towards the floor.

"You can!" Teeny said. "And you will. You're not alone, Mary Jingo. We're here to help you."

Teeny and Corb smiled at Mary in the same way, with sympathy and understanding.

"I know how you feel, a little bit, Mary," Corb said softly and slowly, drawing herself up from the table and straightening her dress. "It is thought to be an honor here to be able to channel or control. Oracles are rare now. Teeny and I were the first to pass the Test in almost twenty years. It is very terrifying to know you have power, but you feel that you will never understand how to use it. We heard about what happened out there when the Flikes were disabled. You are more powerful than you can even imagine."

Mary felt a little cheered up by what the two O.I.T.s had told her. She thought about her best friend Katie then, and how much Katie would love this. She remembered the day before she had come to LeeChee, the two of them riding their bikes down the street. She was lost in thought, when she felt a hard pressure on her hand. She looked up and Teeny and Corb were staring at her with wide eyes.

"How did you do that?" Corb asked suddenly, blinking rapidly.

"Do what?" Mary asked.

"Who was the girl on the bicycle? The yellow-haired one?"

"You could—you could see that?" Mary asked, jumping back and dropping Corb's hand. "That was Katie Sparrow. She's my—my best friend."

"But how?" Teeny asked, her eyes wide and staring.

"I don't know. Corb was holding my hand, I don't know. Did I do something wrong?" Mary asked.

"No, of course not, Mary Jingo!" Corb said quickly. "We'll ask Lady Kathryn about it. She'll know what it means. It's probably some channeling or controlling thing we haven't learned yet."

Mary nodded quickly. These two girls were so much nicer than the girls at her school, but she still wanted them to like her. Corb and Teeny exchanged a look and Teeny said, "Clean clothes live in there."

She pointed towards a closet door that was covered in honeysuckle vines.

"The room is designed to answer to your needs," Corb said, spreading her hands. "So if you would like to take a bath, just focus on the Everything and think about a bathtub and it will appear."

Mary said nothing. She just looked at them.

"We'll see you downstairs soon!" they both said.

The trap door closed behind them and Mary was left alone in her sweet-smelling golden-brown room.

Mary climbed down the stairs, carefully closing the trap door over her head. She had bathed in a tub that had appeared when she had done what Corb had suggested and focused her thoughts on it. She had spent several more minutes than she needed to in the hot water, feeling the hot lava of frustration slip away from her like soap bubbles.

She had found a green dress in the closet Teeny pointed out, similar to the one Corb had been wearing, except her dress had no stripe across the chest. She also found a pair of soft green leggings to match. Her sneakers from the day before had been replaced with a set of heavy leather sandals. When she had tightened a belt at her waist, she had felt a little sad that she did not have a dagger like Corb and Teeny.

At the bottom of the stairs, Mary stood in a curved hallway of white marble. Besides its blinding gleam, it looked like a normal hallway. Doors sat intermittently down the hall, as well as other sets of ladder-like stairs that led up to the ceiling. The walls shown incandescently and sunlight poured in through the windows.

Mary had no idea where to go. She looked to her left and then to her right, but she saw no one. She wandered toward the closest window, as the sound of footsteps clattered off the walls. She saw a little man coming towards her as quickly as he could. He wore a green outfit like Teeny's, but with a slash of rainbow fabrics made up of a hundred colors. It was the same small man who had stood on top of a rocking horse and offered Mary his hand. He seemed to fit better here, with his clothes and his small stature, and his bad habit of not answering questions. Rickface, Mary remembered, that was what Bobble and Mikeala had called him.

"That is my name. Glad you learned it all on your own. It saves us a lot of valuable time with introductions," Rickface said, practically skipping towards her. He showed none of the arthritic movements that she had seen when he had been in her house. "You know, Corb and Teeny are very dear, but they fail to recognize that Luminos is a big City and you are still, regrettably, just a girl from the Shadowlands. You could very well get lost."

"Luminos! We made it," Mary said, her eyes lighting up with understanding. This was Van Clare's home. She added softly to herself. "Wonderful."

"Where did you think you were?" Rickface said, looking up at her. His irregular, mismatched features had not changed, but they looked merrier here. Rickface looked, and smelled for that matter, relaxed. He laughed suddenly. "Yes, well, follow me. There's much to do and never enough time to do it, if you follow my meaning. This is Luminos, the City of Lady Kathryn now, as you've probably heard. She is scheduled to inherit much, much more, but at present the world is positively falling to bits, so it might not happen. We try to keep a happy face on things, as I'm sure you realized. You got to meet the O.I.T.s this morning which means that Cody is taking you seriously. That's a good sign, because the Father is not so understanding, and between you and me, Cody can be a bit rash. Not that Cody is not a supreme being, if you know what I mean of course, strictly in the colloquial sense. He can't even sense thoughts—"

"Wait! Why are you talking so much?" Mary asked, realizing, to her great surprise that this made her feel very angry and she had the urge to tell Rickface. "You wouldn't tell me anything that night in the Shadowlands."

"Well, it is correct and honest that this makes you feel angry," Rickface said, walking quickly in front of Mary, and clicking his fingers as if doing an equation. "I had to be a part of the mystery, Mary. I could not force you to choose the Everything, or it would not have worked, you see. You had to choose the Everything for yourself. In your world, I think they call it 'a leap of faith.' Which is ridiculous because you didn't leap anywhere."

Rickface paused his quick walk and looked up at her with the same golden eyes that Bobble and Mikeala possessed, the ruddy white skin of his face full of wrinkles. "I am sorry. I wish I could have told you more. It would have made everything, erm, easier."

"I forgive you," Mary said softly and laid her hand on the keeper's shoulder.

"There is much to do," Rickface said again, with a small smile. He resumed walking so fast that Mary had to jog a few steps to catch up to him.

Rickface led her down a wide set of stairs. Mary was relieved to finally see some stairs that did not end in a ladder and a trap door. They continued through hallways that were blinding and bright. As they walked, the halls began to fill with People of all colors shapes and sizes. Mary gasped at how many of them looked just like her: beige skin with russet undertones and thick black hair. Luminos was home to anyone and everyone who wanted to travel to its circular walls. This differed from her home city of Charleston. She was the only kid of Chinese descent in her entire grade.

Some of the People wore the same green clothing as Mary and Rickface, slashed with different colors. Others wore the black garb that Mary now came to associate with flikers or Thunderbird riders. Some wore the T-shirts and jeans like Bobble favored, and on and on it went until Mary lost track of the different types of outfits and People she saw.

A few People tried to stop Rickface and ask him questions. He would wave them off in his quick way and say that he had important business. He did this so abruptly that none of the People realized that Mary followed him.

At one open window on a lower level, Mary stopped and stared down at the bustling City. Luminos rose before her in a dazzling way. The City glowed on its own. Rickface had gone a hundred yards ahead of Mary (while still talking), before he realized he had lost his charge and came jogging back down the hall towards her.

"It's wonderful," Mary breathed out, pressing her hands on the windowsill and leaning towards the open window. The whole City smelled alive—deep and moving, the way the outdoors all around it had. She breathed in and watched the People moving in the courtyard below.

"Yes, yes," Rickface said, impatient for them to reach their destination. "It's wonderful. Now, come on! They're waiting for you."

They were indeed waiting for her, out in the courtyard of the building she and Rickface exited. Teeny, Corb, Mikeala, Cody (who now wore a lime green bandana around his black hair), and two other women, talking quietly.

And much to Mary's excitement, Bobble.

"BOBBLE!" she shouted and broke into a run across the stones of the courtyard. The keeper giggled and opened his arms. Mary crashed to her knees and clutched him into a tight hug. She felt Mikeala's hands grasp her shoulders, as the three of them became a group hug.

"I was so worried," Mary said.

"I am all right, little one," he said, stepping back.

"He gave us such a scare," Mikeala said, pushing Bobble's shoulder. "But Heavy Dill was able to patch him up. No hard work or controlling and channeling for a few days, but he'll be okay."

"You sealed my mouth shut!" Bobble replied to Mikeala. "You're lucky I didn't suffocate then and there."

"It was for your own good," Mikeala countered. "If I hadn't, you could be dead, or worse, in Thrall."

Mary looked around at the group, as they all peered back at her with interest. She pushed herself to her feet.

"Where's Van Clare?" she asked, looking around. "And WindRunner?"

Their collective smell was so powerful, that Mary had to stop for a moment to regain her balance. These People (or keepers, in the case of Rickface, Bobble, and Mikeala) could upend walls if they wanted. Mary could sense it. She felt safe and terrified all at the same time.

"Are you alright, Mary Jingo?" Corb asked. She looked so tall, standing between Teeny and Bobble and Mikeala. "You look like you've seen a ghost."

"I'm fine," Mary said, trying to wipe whatever look had crossed her face away. She was not going to tell them that their smell was overwhelming. Cody stepped forward.

"Van Clare is down at the Thunderbird Circles. We are headed that way in a minute, but I wanted to introduce you to some very important People first.

"Mary Jingo, may I present to you Lady Kathryn of Luminos and Flores of, well—," Cody trailed off and looked with a mischievous grin at the other woman, who was very sturdy and had a wave of gold-streaked black hair. "We never got around to finding a title for you, did we? You were always just kind of Flores and it never seemed important. What would like you your title to be? Flores of the Ships? Flores of the Rabble Rousers? Flores of Festdelm? Flores of the Great Big Ocean in the Sky?"

Cody could not be serious about this. Mary was sure.

"I like 'Flores who is a better fliker than Loey Cody,'" the woman replied, to which Teeny snorted and Corb hid a smile behind her hand.

Both Flores and Lady Kathryn were Loey Cody's age, or adults, from Mary's vantage point. Flores was almost as tall as Cody, and wore a pair of dark black breeches, with heavy brown boots that came to her knees. She was thick like she would easily withstand a gale force wind. Her billowy white shirt was accompanied by a red belt and several golden necklaces that set off the light brown color of her skin. Her large brown eyes stared at Mary with intensity. She was the coolest pirate Mary had ever seen.

"Very funny, Flores," the other woman, named Lady Kathryn, said. She wore a long white dress with a sky-blue sash like Teeny's and Corb's. It seemed to blend or mirror the rest of the City. She had pale peach skin, dark hair that fell just to her shoulders, and wide-set, catlike green eyes that beamed at everyone around her. She winked at Mary and said, "Everyone knows Cody isn't a very good fliker to begin with."

"Love of my heart," Cody said to Lady Kathryn, dramatically placing a hand over his chest. "You have no idea how much it hurts when you say things like that."

"I'm sure you'll manage," Kathryn said, to which both Teeny and Corb snorted and laughed.

"Well, Mary Jingo, this is Flores. She has been very keen to meet you, which I think is my mistake to allow her to do so," Cody finished, holding up his hands in surrender. "And this is my wife, Lady Kathryn, Ruler of Luminos and someday Empress of all of LeeChee.

"And also, I am changing my name to 'Cody of the Flycycles' since I suddenly have to prove my worth in front of our guest. I'm the only one left who can build the things anyway," Cody said. Mary was not sure whether he was joking or not.

"Do you like being the Aerial Commander for all of LeeChee?" Flores asked, a smile curling on her mouth. "And also the future Emperor? I'm sure Kathryn and Bonnie Judde could find someone else to take your place if Flycycles are all you really care about."

Cody opened his mouth to reply, but Rickface cut in.

"All right! That's enough! You all never take the world around you seriously. Maybe I should go find Bonnie Judde! He'd keep you all in line," Rickface said, casting threatening looks from one person to the next.

"Don't you mean *Sir* Bonnie Judde? We are discussing titles at the moment," Cody asked, wiping a hand across his bandana. The entire group of them stifled a laugh.

"LeeChee is doomed," Rickface said, dramatically. His lopsided face was contracting with anger, but Mary noted that he didn't smell angry. "This is what happens when the only People left to save us are all under the age of 300—oh never mind! I brought the girl down here, like you asked. Don't get her killed!"

"Get me killed?" Mary murmured, unable to keep the fear out of her voice. She looked at Teeny and Corb for help. They both smiled as Rickface trotted off across the courtyard. The walls of the City loomed huge behind Mary's head. Mary felt like they might actually fall on her.

"I take offense to that, Rickface," Mikeala said, placing her hands on her hips. "Not all of us are babies!"

Rickface made a growling sound from a hundred yards away and waved Mikeala off with his hand.

"Are you coming with me?" Rickface called to the other two keepers. He turned on his heel to start walking back towards the tower that he and Mary had just exited. "Bobble should be resting."

"Yes, yes, we're coming," Mikeala yelled. She grasped Bobble's arm and he wobbled a little on his feet. "We're so glad to see you, Mary Jingo. We'll have to talk later about what you said to the trees."

Bobble came over and tipped a small bow to Mary.

"Don't let these ruffians scare you," Bobble said shakily. "You're more powerful than all of them combined."

Bobble gestured at the rest of the group. Mary leaned down and kissed the keeper on the cheek.

"I'm just glad you're all right," Mary said. Bobble blushed and Mikeala clapped her hands together in delight. They both began walking slowly towards Rickface, who stood impatiently next to the door of the tower, stamping his foot. People weaved around him as if they did not want to get too close to his disquiet.

"Well, that's done," said Cody. He smiled at everyone. "Who's ready?"

"Oh look, Loey. Rickface scared the little grommet," Flores said. Her face was infinitely understanding and kind. "Don't be scared. We need your help today, that's all."

"My help? My help with what?" Mary said, thinking about Van Clare and WindRunner. She would feel safer if they were here.

"We're sorry, Mary Jingo," Kathryn said, putting her hand on Cody's arm. "Cody gets a little bit impatient. We need to explain to her what's going on. She is new to our land, after all."

"Can't it wait? You never know who could be listening," Cody said, looking around and shifting from one foot to the other. People were all around them. "Listen

Mary Jingo, a convoy of Shoeboxians is headed this way. We need you to tell us where they are. Can you do that?"

No, Mary thought. How would she even do such a thing?

"She says no," Teeny said, looking from Mary to Cody with a smile on her face. Mary wished very deeply that everyone would stop reading her mind.

"Sorry," Teeny said to Mary and gave her hand a squeeze.

"Remember our lessons," Lady Kathryn said to Teeny lightly. "It is impolite to express someone's thoughts aloud for them, even if you can hear them."

"Yes, I know," Teeny said, hanging her head, her curls shaking.

"I know you're afraid, Mary Jingo. I think that you deserve to know what we're asking of you. But, unfortunately, I have to agree with my old friend Loey Cody here. Too many could be listening," Flores said, crossing her arms across her chest, her bangles clattering.

"So, we're off then?" Loey Cody said, looking around at the group. She had made it this far. It was only a few more steps in the same direction to keep going. She nodded at the Aerial Commander. Loey Cody and Flores took off walking very quickly towards the gate at the edge of the courtyard. Mary started to follow them, but realized that Lady Kathryn, Corb, and Teeny did not follow after Flores and Loey Cody. Mary turned back to them.

"This is where we leave you for now, Mary Jingo," Corb said, folding her hands together at the waist.

"Wait—why aren't you coming with us?" Mary said, looking at her two new friends.

"We have to stay here and do lessons," Teeny said, twirling one of her curls. "I don't exactly hate lessons, but a mission would be so much cooler."

"We'll have plenty of time for missions in the future," Lady Kathryn said to Teeny. She looked at Mary Jingo. "I look forward to your return. You and I have much to work on together. I am eager to begin your training."

"Training?" Mary asked.

"Yes, Mary Jingo," Corb said, her eyes sparkling, "you're going to be an O.I.T.!"

"Like us!" Teeny added.

"Can we do that now?" Mary asked quietly. "Instead of me trying to find Shoeboxians? They are very scary and, also, um, I am not even sure what Cody is asking me to do."

"Uncertainty is as much a part of the Everything as anything else, Mary Jingo," Lady Kathryn said with a knowing smile. "Oracles know that you must blend your instincts and your knowledge in order to be successful. When in doubt, follow your nose."

Teeny laughed and smiled at Mary. The three women, young and adult, were so kind and warm that Mary wanted to stay with them very badly.

"My husband is a good man and will help you along the way. Flores is very accomplished and I think you will like her very much in time. You have nothing to fear from us."

Mary wondered if Lady Kathryn were the type of oracle who could also read thoughts.

Mary nodded and looked back to where Loey Cody and Flores stood by the gate waiting for her.

"You got this!" Teeny said. "Go on this mission then come back and we'll show you how to make a bucket of water explode without touching it!"

"O.I.T. Teeny!" Lady Kathryn said, with a laugh.

"What?" Teeny said, shrugging her shoulders. Mary smiled at them, and turned towards Loey Cody and Flores, making her way across the courtyard.

"All right," Loey Cody said, clapping his hands together. "Let's go!"

CHAPTER

NINE

Luminos was a city of rings, laid out one around the other, as Mary had been able to see from her vantage point earlier in the day from what she now realized was the leftmost of three tall stone towers that shot up out of the middle of the City like lightning rods. Each tower was a white cylinder with a flat top and sheer white sides of gleaming stone. The middle tower was the tallest. The shorter towers that flanked it were still each as tall as the Washington Monument, which Mary had seen on a summer vacation trip with her family last year. The rings around the Towers were not elevated. They lay flat on the ground as if the City had begun at the Towers and grown outward, one circle at a time.

Mary followed Loey Cody and Flores the pirate through the first ring of the City, feeling very lost and unsure of herself, but also excited about becoming an O.I.T. Would she be able to turn a white room into a beautiful display of honeysuckles? She hoped it would be true.

"Okay, Mary Jingo," Loey Cody said to her as they walked through the gate. "Van Clare told me that you are a very strong person and that hiking though the wilds near the mountains was no trouble for you. We're in for a long walk, but I think you can handle it. We're about two hours from the edge of the City."

"In the old days," Flores said, looking over at Mary as they walked on, "we used to fly from the landing circles to the Towers, but your Commander here doesn't allow that anymore."

"It is a safety precaution. We don't know what weapons Mellie has at her disposal," Loey Cody said to his friend.

"Also—the Thunderbirds make a mess!" Flores said with a nod and a wink.

Mary laughed at this then looked up at Cody's very serious face. He did not seem amused, then a smile cracked across his face.

"The Everything is stronger when People are living closely together," Loey Cody explained to Mary. "Kat and I talked about it for a long, long time. It is safer to make sure People are living together on the ground. It does cause its own sort of problems, but it keeps us safe.

"That being said, stay close to us, Mary," he said. "You never know who is watching or listening."

Mary nodded at him and they began walking at a very fast pace. As they walked through the gate, Mary gasped. This City was alive.

The walls of the second ring were made of white stone that shimmered against the sunlight. In each direction, giant murals spanned from the bottom of the wall to the top, showing giant landscapes and Flikes and Thunderbirds and other animals Mary could not name. Semicircle houses were attached to the interior wall, facing towards the giant murals and a broad walking path. Many People had small gardens in front of their houses, so that trees occasionally shaded the walkway. The houses were interrupted by schools and offices and bicycle and Flycycle repair shops. The walkways were crowded with People, carts, and animals all going about their daily business. Against the muraled wall were street vendors selling everything from food to clothing to gadgets. And bicycles. Bicycles were everywhere.

Some of the People stopped to look at Loey Cody and point. A few men and women in the black fliers' garb placed the flat of their palms to their foreheads as they passed. Cody nodded towards them. One woman came to him and grasped his hand. He laid a hand on her shoulder and wished her well.

"This always happens," Flores said to Mary. "You bring the future Emperor down to the streets and everyone stares.

"They are five rings in Luminos. The outer walls glow blue at night," Flores continued as if walking through a crowded City with the most important man in the country were no big deal. They tried to keep to the main thoroughfare that led from one gate to the next. A system of lights hung between the gates and the rings themselves that reminded Mary very much of stoplights. Flores pointed to them.

"Pretty nifty, huh? Bonnie Judde installed these a few years ago. They let People know when to stop. And when to go. They have very much helped with bicycle accidents."

"Cool," Mary said. "We have something like this in the Shadowlands."

Loey Cody looked at her sharply and said nothing. The light above them turned green and they began walking again.

"It's so busy," Mary said with a gasp. Loey Cody had promised her a long walk, but it was going by very quickly with so much to see and hear and smell. As they moved into the next ring, they passed People sitting on the ground, looking tired and hungry.

"The outer-most ring of the City used to be strictly for markets and merchants—no one lived here," Flores continued. "But we're growing again, with People fleeing from towns in Thrall. They just show up here, not sure of what happened or where they came from. We're doing our best to help them, but this has been a very hard time for us."

Mary felt deeply sad for these People. This City was so alive. She imagined Greenberg, the town that she had seen when she had first arrived, teeming with life and energy like this. Instead it had been cold, and sad, and terrifying. Is this what the People of LeeChee had given up for fear?

The fifth ring of Luminos was huge, wide enough that it would take a solid wall of fifty Thunderbirds to block it. The doors of the gate out of fourth ring and into the fifth ring were heavy and ominous. A couple of Thunderbirds sat on perches next to the walls. Mary could smell their fierce wildness before they were even within earshot of their cackling voices. They came to swift attention as Cody waked through the gate. Their wings and bodies were hard and scaly, like WindRunner's, but their patterns were made up of different shapes. The Thunderbirds stayed at attention until Cody was a few paces closer to being outside the walls of the City, at which point their cackling began again.

Flores had just told Mary that this ring was for shops and merchants. On the far wall, a giant mural of Cody and Kathryn's faces was painted, with the words "LIVE FREE FOREVER" above them. The mural version of Cody's eyes were so yellow-gold, they seemed to blot out the blinding white light of the City.

"Mmm—this one never gets old," Flores said, crossing her arms and looking at the giant portrait of

Cody and Kathryn. "You know, one of these days, I'm going to come down here with a can of paint and draw mustaches on both of you."

"I think Kathryn would love that," Loey Cody said genuinely, looking up at the mural. All around it, People sat on the ground, most of them looking cold and hungry. Cody crossed the space to a family of four and squatted down in front of them. Mary was too far away to hear their conversation. She looked all around her, to the shops surrounding the inner wall of the ring to the brilliant blue sky above. The shops were marked by signs that featured names like "Real Flycycles Repair" or "Green Eatz."

"I need to speak with the Father. We're going to have to set up a new camp for refugees. They're overflowing any space we have left," Loey Cody said to Flores, who nodded in response. The sadness in his voice struck Mary very deeply in her soul. For a moment, she smelled the stink of the Shoeboxians in her nose.

Cody and Flores collected Flikes from Real Flycycle Repair, and Cody paid the owner. She put up a fight in taking Cody's money, but he finally convinced her and placed some coins in her hand.

"Why didn't you just use the disappearing thing for these?" Mary asked, looking at the Flycycles. "I forgot what Van Clare called it."

"The dissipator?" Loey Cody asked her. She nodded. "They haven't made a dissipator powerful enough to hold all of my Flikes. And I can't walk around with fifteen of them on my belt, now can I?"

Flores very notably rolled her eyes. Mary laughed to herself. For some reason, in that moment, Loey Cody reminded her very much of her own dad and all of the junk in their garage.

"It also gives me a chance to check on how things are going in the City," Loey Cody said. "I need to talk to People, or I will lose track of what is going on."

Cody's Flike was a deep electric blue. It was a full-suspension mountain bike, but it's fork and handlebars were lighter weight. The black box over his back tire was the smallest Mary had yet seen, and Flores eyed it with suspicion. Her Flike was big and instantly reminded Mary of a motorcycle. It was a shining gray color with chrome handlebars and tire covers. It looked menacing. Mary wanted to take a step back from it.

They waved goodbye to the shop owner and made their way through the imposing gates of Luminos.

People streamed around them in and out of the gates. Once they were outside the walls standing on the wide flat road into the City, Mary gasped in shock. The City was surrounded by flat, blue, grassy plains for as far as her eye could see. A little ways beyond the bright blue expanse, trees began to appear and grew taller as they reached the foot of the mountains. Mary could almost see the mountains in the bright sunlight. She desperately stared, trying to make out clear edges. The harder she tried, the less of them she could see.

"Are you okay?" Flores asked her.

"Yes," Mary said quietly. "It's just, well, the grass is blue."

"Sure it is!" Flores said, looking around.

"We don't have blue grass in the Shadowlands."

"At some point, Mary Jingo, you will have to tell me all the weird and wonderful things about the Shadowlands," Flores said with a laugh. She saddled her Flike and looked upward. "I need to head up to the ship, check in with Makeen, and make sure they have not seen any unusual activity."

Without warning, she launched into the air with a 'woohoo!'

"Sure!" Cody called after her. "That's fine! Take off wherever! Whatever you need to do!"

He looked back at Mary.

"She never listens," he said with a smile. "We've been friends since the Test, and no matter my rank or her rank, she still treats me like we're eleven."

He sighed and turned towards Mary. He sounded exasperated, but she could see the smile in his eyes.

"This will be your first verbal lesson in Fliking. You cannot just takeoff and land wherever you like. No matter what you see People like Flores do. Come on."

He and Mary made their way along the road. To the left and the right were two large circles, branching off. Mary felt a familiar feeling in her stomach. They looked exactly like the ones she had seen in Greenberg. Except these circles were teeming with People.

"Wait!" she exclaimed, the pieces clicking together. "I've seen these before!"

"Have you?" Cody asked, cocking his head to the side.

"Yes! When I um, woke up here. In LeeChee. I was in a bunch of big, rolling hills. And I walked a little ways and found a town. And it was brown and smelled very bad. But it had two of these circle thingies outside of it. And I walked down to one and fell asleep. And then Van Clare, and Bobble and Mikeala and WindRunner found me."

"Interesting," Cody said, putting a finger to his chin. They were almost to the intersection where the road split off towards one of the circles. The shops along the outside ring were so busy that Mary couldn't make out anything beyond them. Cody continued, "Van Clare said that she found you outside of Greenberg, but you were not in the city. You said it was brown?"

"Yes," Mary nodded, feeling like she had said too much. "It was very brown. Even the air was brown. It was honestly gross."

"Van Clare was right," Loey Cody said, as if he just put the pieces together for himself. "You are perfect for this mission."

Mary nodded. She was not sure what that meant. They were in the outer ring of the circle now. It was surprisingly orderly, with People and their Flikes lined up towards the inner circle. Mary now realized that the yellow lines divided the large roadway to keep traffic going in only one direction on either side of the street. If someone tried to cross or stepped on the lines, they glowed blinding and bright. Up ahead, Mary could just make out the giant black wings of Thunderbirds. Suddenly, one launched itself from the ground and took off in the sky.

She and Cody joined the line of People. A woman in Thunderbird garb approached him, touched the flat of her palm to her forehead and said, "Commander Cody, you don't need to wait here. I can escort you to the front of the line."

"That's okay, Praneet," he said, flashing a wide smile at the rider. "Thank you for the offer, but my O.I.T. friend here and I are happy to wait alongside everyone else. But, if you don't mind, can you please let Captain Van Clare know that we're here?"

"Absolutely, I can do that," Praneet said. She saluted Cody again and made off through the gates towards where Mary could just make out Thunderbird wings.

"What's the point of being Commander if you don't go to the front of the line?" Mary said, very quietly. It was a joke that Katie would make. It was a braver joke than Mary.

"What did you say? Did you just make a joke?" Cody said. Mary looked up at Loey Cody. His eyes were piercing, but the kindness in his face reminded her of her own father again. She should tell him now, before she let them all down and ruined everything.

"Mr. Cody, I mean, Commander Cody, sir. So, I don't want to upset you, but I'm not cut out for this mission. I don't know how I ended up here, but I have friends at home, well, my best friend for one, and my brother Sam, they would be better cut out for these missions. I'm not brave. I'm not anything, really. I disabled all the Flikes when we were coming back... I don't know what I'm doing here..."

Mary trailed off, she didn't know what else to say. She stared at the ground, at Cody's sneakers (*How did he get sneakers here?*), at the blue grass below them.

"Do you want to go home, Mary Jingo?"

"I don't, I don't... I don't know," she said, twisting her hands and not looking at him. Cody rubbed his hand down his face and smiled.

"When I was eight, my mom went out sailing with the Rabble Rousers, those are Flores' and my mother's People. It wasn't a dangerous journey or even an out of the ordinary one, but somehow, she disappeared. My father was beside himself. He cried for weeks. One morning, he came to my room and told me that we were leaving. We had family in Luminos and we weren't going to stay on the borders of Festdelm anymore. He said that being so close to the Great Big Ocean Sky was too terrible for him. Too many memories. We boarded a boat and came here. I was so angry. I loved that little town outside of Festdelm. All of my friends were there. I didn't want to leave. Plus, I had to go to work because we didn't have very much money. So, I started building things. Small things at first, like a ramp for my toy bicycles, and a set of stairs to help my granny get into bed. And do you know what? I was good at it. Me. I was. A poor boy from Festdelm was good at building things."

"I'm sorry you lost your mom," Mary said quietly.

Mary looked up at Cody. His face held so much kindness and warmth, she wanted to wrap her arms around his neck.

"What else did you build?"

"That's the point, Mary Jingo," Loey Cody said with a smile. "Sometimes you end up somewhere you don't expect to be or don't want to be. But my dad always says that you have to bloom where you're planted. Find your gifts and use them," he paused to stand as the line moved forward. He looked to his left and right, to make sure no one around them was listening.

"We won't force you to stay. Rickface is a powerful keeper, he can find a way to escort you back to your hometown. But we talked to your parents and they're okay with you being here. I think for myself (and I don't want to speak for anyone else), we would be very happy to have you stay. So you can see what you are made of."

Mary's jaw dropped open. She took a step forward next to Cody as the line moved again.

"What do you mean, you talked to my parents?"

"Well, of course we did. We weren't going to have you go missing in the middle of the night. Can you imagine what they would have thought?" Cody smiled. "Rickface talked to them. From what I've heard, it went really badly at first, but he eventually was able to get them to come around. You can talk to them when we get back to the tower. Rickface found a way—"

At this Mary threw her arms around Cody and hugged him. To everyone standing nearby, the Commander looked startled at first. Then he hugged Mary back with his free arm that was not holding his Flike. When Mary pushed back, she looked up at Cody and laughed. She could clearly picture Rickface standing on her coffee table and explaining where Mary had gone. Of course, he would stand on the coffee table, as he seemed to like to stand on furniture. Her mother would be so angry that he dared to put his feet on her furniture.

"Thank you, Mr. Cody," she said quietly. She added quickly, "Sir."

"Now, I will ask you again. Do you want to go home?"

Mary shook her head.

"What was that?"

"No," she said. "I don't want to go home."

At that moment, she smelled it. Every lovely and perfect thing that she loved the most. She felt a sense of purpose surge through her and, for just a moment, she did not feel afraid, as if something propped her up and held her tightly. Cody looked at her and smiled, and laughed. He laughed a big, loud laugh. Everyone in line turned and stared, then smiles broke out across all of their faces. They had reached one of the ticketing booths. Mary looked behind the glass of the booth and saw Praneet, who spoke briefly with Cody and waved them through.

CITY OF LIGHTS

Cody told her that they were going to the fourth quarter of the innermost circle, which was for Thunderbird takeoffs. Mary now realized what purpose the four quarters served. The paved ones were for Flikes; one side for arrivals and one side for departures. The grassy quarters were for Thunderbirds; one side for arrivals and one side for departures. As the skirted the split-rail fence, Mary watched as Flikes of all colors, shapes, and sizes took off and landed around them. A Flycycle with twelve seats landed not too far from Mary, and People began to disembark. She wondered how something like that could fly.

"Those are public," Cody said, pointing at the twelve-seater. "The Emperor's grandfather started them. They go from one city to another and leave several times a day."

She only nodded and kept moving. Behind the circle, she saw tall trees and raised platforms like she had seen at Greenberg, except these were not empty. Great Thunderbirds of varying sizes sat atop them, chatting with each other and cawing loudly. Most of them were jet black, like WindRunner, but a few had brightly colored feathers that shimmered and changed in the afternoon sunlight.

"Commander, why are those Thunderbirds multicolored?"

"They're not wearing any armor. It is kind of shocking, I guess, the first time you see an unarmored Thunderbird. I remember when I was twelve and it happened to me. My friend SpearWing landed in front of me, and he was every color of the rainbow. I almost didn't recognize him."

"Wow! I wonder what WindRunner looks like without armor."

"You'll see him eventually," Cody said, and shrugged his shoulders. "A lot of them don't like it—the armor, I mean. They say it's heavy and impedes their legs, which is important to their balance when they fly. But it's what their High Chief commands, so they all wear it."

"Like a uniform."

"Exactly. Here we are!"

They came to a large opening in the split-rail fence. A large number 4 was painted on a post next to the opening. Through the quarter, men and women hurried past in plaid pants and printed T-shirts, directing Thunderbirds and riders where to go.

The riders wore all black with helmets under their arms, or golden goggles pushed up into their hair. Next to some of them were Thunderbirds, standing on their four legs, readying themselves for takeoff. A few of the Thunderbirds stared at Mary curiously, smelling wildly ferocious, but not unfriendly. She followed Cody past Thunderbirds and riders and jumped as someone grabbed her shoulder.

"Watch where you step, missy," a familiar voice said. "If you step on someone's tail, you'll be in big trouble."

"VAN CLARE!" Mary shouted, as she gave Van Clare a hug.

"Hey kid," she replied, her hair perfectly mowhawked again, and her uniform spotless. "You get enough rest? I know it's been a big few days."

"I'm fine. I'm so glad to see you, I have so much to tell you."

"It's the little warrior, again," another familiar rumbling voice said. Mary looked up and saw WindRunner snapping his huge beak through the air as his body shook with laughter. Mary was overcome with his smell of wildness and merriment. Mary hugged the great Thunderbird's neck.

I missed you, she said, across the Mindspan.

Who me? he replied with a laugh.

Mary released the Thunderbird's neck to see Loey Cody and another man walking towards them. The man was small, around Cody's age, with pinched rat-like features, and waxy pale white skin. He wore a gray three-piece suit that gleamed in the morning light. His hair was a sandy brown color and slicked away from his face like a gangster in one the movies Sam liked to watch without permission.

"So," he said, in a loud booming voice. "This is the warrior whom we were promised!"

"Hi," Mary said weakly. The man and Cody were standing in front of them now. Cody had his hands clasped behind his back and rocked a few times on his heels. His Flike was nowhere in sight.

"Mary Jingo, meet Bonnie Judde. He is the Emperor's right-hand man and is here to help us with this mission," Loey Cody said, his mouth forming a thinner line than normal.

"How do you do, Miss Jingo?" Bonnie Judde said with a sweeping bow. He was much shorter than Cody and Van Clare, but taller than Mary or the average keeper. He looked towards Van Clare. "The Father and Heavy Dill send their regrets, Van Clare. They wanted to make it but are busy at work."

"What? Why are you talking about my dads? I had breakfast with them a few hours ago" Van Clare said. "They never come to see me off on missions."

"Aw, I see," Bonnie Judde said, making a tut-tut sound with his tongue. "Well, that's a shame. I thought they'd want to see you off on such a big day."

Van Clare smiled tightly. Mary could see her disappointment.

"You should get started, Van Clare," Loey Cody said gently. "Your dads know that you go on special missions all the time. They would have to be down here every day if they came to see you off for all of them."

Van Clare nodded.

"I guess you and Mary are taking WindRunner?" Bonnie Judde said. "I'll be going on LightningChaser. We need to hurry, we don't want to be out past dark."

"You won't be taking me anywhere," WindRunner said shortly. "I have volunteered to carry Mary Jingo and the Captain myself."

"Right, right, my apologies," Bonnie Judde said. "I'll see you in the sky."

He sauntered off towards the biggest Thunderbird Mary had seen yet. If that was LightningChaser, they looked like a very powerful Thunderbird.

Loey Cody watched Bonnie Judde walk away.

"Why is he coming with us?" Van Clare asked Cody, a pained look on her face.

"I have to agree," WindRunner said. "I don't generally speak ill of other members in the Thunderbird Corps, but LightningChaser is known to be very unpredictable."

"Listen," Loey Cody said. "I don't like it either, but Bobble and Mikeala are not able to fly and you need someone who can channel and control on this mission. If something gets out of hand, you will need help. And Bonnie Judde is a good fighter, even if he is not a lot of fun to be around. "

"What is the mission?" Mary asked. She had been wondering this for several hours now, and had finally found the moment to ask.

"Van Clare will tell you above," Loey Cody said. "I hate to keep all these secrets, but Van Clare can explain that too."

"All right, we'll be fine," Van Clare said as she handed Mary a pair of golden goggles. "Here. You're riding in front. WindRunner is certain he can carry both of us, but he is going to tell us if we've flown too high or too far. Right, WindRunner?"

"Yes, yes," WindRunner said, snapping his beak over his shoulder towards Van Clare.

"Good luck," Cody said. "May the Everything protect you."

"Wait—you're not coming with us?" Mary asked Cody, as Van Clare helped hook her feet into the restraints.

"No, Mary Jingo. I need to Flike out to the Barns where we do all the Flycycle repair. They need my help this morning. You're in good hands," the Aerial Commander touched his palm to his forehead, as Van Clare jumped up on WindRunner's back behind Mary and pulled her goggles down over her eyes. She mimicked Loey Cody's gesture and told WindRunner she was ready over the Mindspan.

Okay, Mary. This time we fly together, Van Clare's voice came in crystal clear in Mary's mind. Mary hung on to the handholds as WindRunner flexed his legs, waited for the signal, and jumped into the sky.

CHAPTER
TEN

The wind rushed past Mary's hair and ears. WindRunner was flying much faster than he had a few nights ago when they set off from Greenberg. Just to their right, through thick cloud embankments, they could make out LightningChaser, who was setting the pace for their breakneck speed.

Cody seemed... I don't know. Weird? Mary said to Van Clare. She had just finished telling the Thunderbird Captain about waking up in the room high in the left tower of Luminos. Van Clare had laughed at her descriptions of Teeny and Corb, but had gone completely silent when she mentioned her

O.I.T. training. Mary kept talking and told her about her, Cody, and Flores' walk through the City and how Flores reminded her of Crazy Aunt Caroline, her dad's sister. It was easy to talk to Van Clare, to tell her everything that had happened. Mary continued, *He is always looking around, like someone is going to jump on him.*

Van Clare's laugh tinkled over the Mindspan.

I know. My dad often says that Cody has become paranoid. But I think it's with good reason. Mellie always seems to know what we're planning, where we're headed. Cody is worried someone is giving away our plans.

Really?

Yes—even with the mission to come get you. I did it in secret, and um, not necessarily with permission. And somehow, she knew right where to find us. It's strange.

Mary thought this over for a moment. What Van Clare had just told her made her fearful. She felt a cold hand grip her stomach. Mary suddenly felt pressure on her mind, as if someone were knocking and would like to come in. She heard a thin voice say,

Hello, Captain Van Clare and Mary Jingo! Can I join your little soirée?

Mary recognized the voice. She had heard it at the landing circle. She looked over and Bonnie Judde was standing (yes, standing) on LightningChaser's back and waiving his arm over his head at them.

Well met, Bonnie Judde, Van Clare replied. Mary looked over her shoulder and saw Van Clare release one of the handholds long enough to place her palm to her forehead in Bonnie Judde's direction.

So, have you told the little grom what we're doing up here? Bonnie Judde asked. Even across the Mindspan, his voice sounded like a sneer.

I haven't had the time, Van Clare replied smoothly. *You are welcome to do the honors, Oracle Judde.*

Don't mind if I do, he replied. Mary gripped the handholds tighter and tried to keep her thoughts quiet as she listened. *Mary Jingo, I heard that you met our foe Mellie in the forest the other night. She is nasty, isn't she? I'm sure our friend Van Clare told you that the Everything is shrinking and towns are under Thrall. But we're not quite sure how she's doing it. Or what is becoming of the Everything as it shrinks.*

Bonnie Judde paused here, as if Van Clare or Mary should ask a question. Mary followed Van Clare's lead and remained silent. Up ahead, the clouds began to clear and Mary could see shimmering peaks. They were headed for the mountains. Bonnie Judde continued.

A rather large group of Shoeboxians is camped just over the mountains. We know it because our Scouts keep finding tracks and dead animals all over the place. But we don't know where they are or where they are headed. That is where you come in.

Me? Mary thought with a shock. *Me? How am I supposed to know where they are or where they are headed?*

That's just it, Mary Jingo, Van Clare said calmly. *We think that you might be able to find them, by, well, using your nose.*

What? Mary said.

If I may, Bonnie Judde said. His voice was nasally even over Mindspan. *Some oracles can use the Everything empathetically to sense threats, emotions, and intentions. It's a function of channeling. You seem to be able to do this, based on reports, with a sense of smell. With proper training, you'll be able to harness this ability. But for now, we need you to seek out this band of Shoeboxians and see where they are headed.*

They were so close to the mountains now. The wind became colder and Mary could feel her teeth begin to chatter. She regretted that she wore sandals.

What am I supposed to do? Mary asked, trying to think about what it meant that she could smell intentions.

Think back to the other night, Bonnie Judde said. *Think back to the way the Shoeboxians smelled. Think and focus and see if you can smell anything.*

How… how? Mary stammered inside her own mind. *How did you know that I could smell… um… things?*

Bonnie Judde's cold laugh pierced the Mindspan.

Oh, great Shadowlands warrior, you do not guard your thoughts well. You've been telling WindRunner, Bobble, and Mikeala for days all about your special ability. But don't worry. This is going to help us. You're helping us!

Mary shivered against the cold air. They crested the mountains and Mary tried not to look down. They had been able to read her thoughts? As a shy person this was Mary's worst nightmare. She felt like screaming. She wanted to tell WindRunner to land. To take her home. Anything, anything other than knowing that these People had been listening to her innermost thoughts.

Just then, she felt a strong, wild presence press at the edge of her conscious.

It's okay, Mary. I'm your friend. You can trust me. I'm going to take care of you, WindRunner's voice echoed through the chamber of Mary's mind. WindRunner glided along and pushed good thoughts and feelings her way. *They can't hear us, Mary Jingo. I have shielded our conversation from Judde and Van Clare.* Mary did not answer him, even in her mind, she could not find words to put to all of her feelings.

Don't worry, little one. I know you feel betrayed. The Resistors meant no harm. They deeply need help. This was not the best way to get it.

What do I do, WindRunner? she thought, helplessly.

You help them, or you do not. But LeeChee is fading. If the Thrall continues, the Everything will disappear completely. And then, who knows? The land may cease to exist all together. Cody feared to tell you this much. We have been betrayed so many times. He cares so deeply to save what he loves.

Mary did not know what to do. They were almost over the edge of the mountains. She could just start to see the tops of trees that saved her life a few nights before. The flowers in the field, the trees of the forest—she had seen so many beautiful things here already.

Will you stay with me, WindRunner? The thought was so faint, it was barely a whisper. She gripped the handholds of his armor harder as an anxious knot formed in her stomach.

As long as my wingtips can catch the breeze, as long as my claws can clasp a branch, I swear to you, Mary Jingo of the Shadowlands, you can always count on me.

As he said the words, a jet of golden light burst forth from WindRunner's beak. She could feel

WindRunner at the edge of her mind. She somehow knew in her heart that something powerful had happened when he swore to protect her. That the Everything had sealed their bond.

He arced through the sky. Laughing across the Mindspan, he yelled *HOLD ON!* as he did a giant loop in the sky.

Mary had ridden only one rollercoaster in her life and this was much, much worse. Her stomach dropped to her toes and surged up again, her feet pulling against the restraints. WindRunner must have dropped the shield around their Mindspan, as Mary could now hear Van Clare laughing, whooping, and screaming, *MARY JINGO, ARE YOU OKAY?* all at once.

Once they were level to the ground again, and Mary had just barely caught her breath, Mary glanced over at Bonnie Judde, who still stood on LightningChaser's back and shook his head.

Are you quite finished? he asked. *Now, Mary Jingo, as I was saying, what do you smell?*

You got this Mary, Van Clare said. *Just focus, at least, that's what my dad always used to tell me when he tried to teach me how to channel or control. I was hopeless, but you get the idea. Just tell us what you smell.*

Okay, I can try, Mary said. She closed her eyes and took a deep breath. She could feel WindRunner bolstering her across their bond, giving her strength.

What did she smell? She smelled WindRunner's wildness and ferocity and the strength of their newly formed bond. She smelled Van Clare—all cold steel and hard strength, like a sword blade. Something slightly rotten slipped past her nose too, like garbage that had sat in the can for too many summer days. It was there as quickly as it was gone. She reached out further. She could smell LeeChee. It smelled alive, growing. It reminded her of the school field trip she went on to the marshes around Charleston. The whole place had been alive and fragrant, life and death all in one place. She kept searching, breathing deeper and deeper, until it hit her senses. The angry, evil stink of the Shoeboxians. Off to their right, in the forest, Mary could smell it.

"They're there," Mary said aloud. She then focused her thoughts and said again, *They're over there. To our right. A whole lot of Shoeboxians. A whole, whole lot. And…*

She stopped suddenly. A different smell filled the air. A hole in the forest where the Everything did not exist. And something else had taken its place. Something terrible.

Oh no, she said.

What is it? Van Clare asked, urgency in her voice across the Mindspan.

The Everything. It's—I don't know how to describe it—it has changed.

What do you mean? she heard Bonnie Judde say.

Give her a moment, WindRunner commanded. He was flying in the direction where Mary had smelled the Shoeboxians. Mary realized that he followed what she sensed through their bond. LightningChaser was forced to follow in the smaller Thunderbird's wake.

Mary focused on the smell. It wasn't quite like the butterfly that Rickface has released in her attic all those nights ago, but it was close. Close enough that Mary could hardly tell the difference. It smelled almost like all the best things. All the most wonderful things that she had ever smelled, kind of. The smells were off by a hair. Like chocolate chip cookies that had just started to burn, or fresh cut poisonous grass. It stopped her in her tracks.

Beneath us, there is a rather large number of Shoeboxians, Mary said. *But something else. I can't tell you what it is. It smells like... like...,* Mary trailed off.

Bonnie Judde and LightningChaser were now flying wing to wing with WindRunner. Mary could see Bonnie Judde's eyes glinting behind his golden goggles.

Mellie is definitely down there, Mary said, closing her eyes tight and breathing in deeply through her nose. She caught Mellie's specific decaying smell along with the Shoeboxian odor. It had been there all along. She just had not named it. The other smell bothered her. Tickled her nose. It made her want to go find it and experience it. It was that good, even if it did smell a little false. *But—I don't know! It smells like… the Everything. I think. But not really. It smells wonderful—like the Everything does—but it's not the Everything. I think. I mean, the Everything could have changed? Does it do that?*

She became distracted as pictures began to flash through her brain that coincided with the smells. She could see Shoeboxians sitting on the ground, their legs splayed out in front of them. They picked their teeth and farted loudly. It made Mary want to vomit. She clapped her hand over her forehead.

Maybe it is as we feared, Bonnie Judde said, with real fear in his voice. *Mellie has a weapon we cannot defeat.*

No! Van Clare shouted, cutting through the wave of defeat that spread through the group. *I won't accept that. The Everything protect me. WindRunner, take us lower.*

Mary! Bonnie Judde shouted, alarmed. *What is it?*

I'm seeing—I'm seeing..., Mary trailed off.

Her heart pounded heavily in her chest. She barely noticed as WindRunner took wide circles above the encampment. She was transported somewhere else. Pictures and images flashed in front of her vision so quickly, that she could not tell her friends what she saw.

Underneath Mary, WindRunner and the rest, the camp stretched out in all directions. It seemed to go on for a very great and unpredictable distance. Van Clare and Bonnie Judde discussed numbers over the Mindspan, trying to calculate the force. This was made harder as they watched Shoeboxians running from tent to tent. They were preparing to move. Mary listened to them half-heartedly as they flew past. The camp was rank with Shoeboxian smell. Mary felt herself growing faint.

But where are they going? Van Clare wondered aloud. *I see so many of them.*

It's an invasion force, Bonnie Judde said, not looking at her. *This is worse than we thought.*

It's too late, Mary said quietly over the Mindspan. *They've seen us.*

What's that? WindRunner said, turning his massive head slightly to one side.

They've seen us, WindRunner. They know we're up here, she replied weakly.

Her heart wasn't in it, but it didn't matter. As if to confirm her statements, a black mass began to rise in the sky and burst into a thousand pellets. They were just like the ammunition Van Clare had slung off her bike chain two nights before. Mary's arms flew up to her face. WindRunner let out a mighty call and flew rapidly backwards, turning his armored underbelly towards the pellets. Mary had to grapple for the hand-holds near his shoulder joints in order to hold on and heard Van Clare do the same. To their left, Bonnie Judde whipped his hands through the air, gathering golden light towards him. He threw a shield in front of LightningChaser and another in front of WindRunner.

Mary tried to cover her face and hold on to WindRunner at the same time. The explosion of the black pellets on Bonnie Judde's shield were loud and distracting. Her vision flashed again and she felt woozy in her seat. The air around her screamed in her ears, building louder and louder.

WE HAVE TO GET OUT OF HERE! she screamed desperately.

Van Clare let out a solid cry and WindRunner, already in mid-circle, broke formation from LightningChaser and turned around, wheeling back toward Luminos. Just as the two Thunderbirds came back together, Mary knew what was coming, because she had seen it. She didn't have the words to warn her friends. The words froze in her mouth. Behind them, the barrage of pellets had stopped. Bonnie Judde pointed across LightningChaser's back as a single reddish trail arced into the blue sky. It reminded Mary of fireworks or bottle rockets in July. It was almost beautiful.

On my mark, Van Clare screamed. *Fly full-out…NOW!*

The red spark exploded as the Thunderbird's wings beat mightily against the wind, making Mary's hair fly back and forcing her to grab at the handholds. She couldn't tell what was forcing them forward—WindRunner's effort or the explosion. She tried not to look back. But then, the smell—like all the almost best things in the world. Like the Everything, but not the

Everything. But close enough—she looked over her shoulder and saw a coppery-colored cloud following them. It seemed not to hurry, but also to have no problem keeping speed. It flashed up images of things that Mary liked. That she appreciated. The things that she wanted, but hadn't gotten yet. In fact, Mary very much liked this coppery cloud. She started to stretch towards it, and it slowly seemed to creep a little closer to WindRunner's tail. Mary even willed it a little closer. Look at that shiny Flike! She could see herself with it. Standing in her front yard, while Katie rode by on just a silly, simple bicycle, green with envy.

The others were turning too. The Thunderbirds seemed to slow down, even though their wings were still moving. Van Clare's face was bright and sunny, smiling at the cloud. She asked WindRunner to slow down. And then commanded it.

"I'm the leader of a division, aren't I?" she shouted, standing up dangerously on WindRunner's back. She teetered a little and sucked her teeth. "I never get any respect."

Don't feel sorry for her! Mary heard WindRunner say in her mind. Mary returned her gaze to the cloud. WindRunner continued, *She is trying to be a hero. And heroes get what they deserve. These humans all think they're better than the rest of us anyway.*

Mary didn't know if she agreed with WindRunner or not. Her thoughts jumbled together as she looked at the bronze cloud. It had started to hiss at her, at all of them, but no one seemed to notice.

"Whatcha doing, Bonnie Judde?" Van Clare yelled. Bonnie Judde and LightningChaser went closer to the cloud. Mary felt Van Clare teeter dangerously close to WindRunner's tail. WindRunner shouted over the air, telling her to stop with the madness. "Are you trying to be honorable? Old, honorable Bonnie Judde. You're not that great, Judde, no matter what the Emperor says about you. Well, I got news for you, you're not that honorable. You're not as honorable as me. And you're surely not as brave. You just fly right over to that stupid cloud and see what happens! I bet nothing happens. Not one useful thing."

Van Clare continued and Mary found that she agreed with the Thunderbird Captain. Bonnie Judde had been nothing but rude to her since they had met.

Bonnie Judde didn't look back at them. He flew straight up to the cloud and asked LightningChaser to stop. Long tendrils of the cloud reached out toward

Bonnie Judde. Mary knew, instantly, that if he just flew into the cloud—he might have any wish in LeeChee granted. His head cocked to the side and Mary felt instantly jealous that Bonnie Judde had thought of this before her. What had she been thinking? She should have been the first one to go out to the cloud! Van Clare yelled louder and louder—and was now so dangerously close to falling off WindRunner. Mary hardly noticed. She stared intently at Bonnie Judde and resented his ideas.

"Go away," Bonnie Judde said to the copper cloud, his voice amplified over the air. It was not a request, but it was not a demand. It was just a simple command. And for a split second, the potent almost-Everything smell broke apart. Mary saw the entire situation clearly. Bonnie Judde radiated with a powerful smell that made Mary's heart cheer for him. The gap closed and she felt all heavy and resentful again.

"We don't know what you are," Bonnie Judde said, just as evenly and as calmly. "And we don't accept you here. Go away. Now. And don't ever come back."

The cloud contracted and hissed violently. Van Clare exhaled and then yelped, as she realized where she stood. Bonnie Judde was blown back a little, but he held on. Mary could smell him through the haze. He was terribly powerful. His Thunderbird radiated too. Just as powerful.

"GO! NOW!" Bonnie Judde said, raising his hands palms up. They were glittering softly gold and the air around him began to vibrate. The cloud contracted again and hissed like it was laughing. The voice of Mellie floated through the air, as if she stood in the center of the cloud itself.

"Is this the best you have, Bonnie Judde? Bonnie Judde—boy born to nothing. No friends, no powers, no future. You think the Emperor loves you? As soon as you make a mistake, he won't need you anymore. You're pitiful, you know. And everyone around you knows it. They see it in your eyes. They feel it when they talk to you. Poor, pitiful Bonnie Judde. Doesn't got what everybody else has got. That's why they promoted you, you know? It wasn't because of your skills. It was because they all felt sorry for you. Poor, pitiful, Bonnie Judde."

Bonnie Judde's powerful smell waned.

Mary felt her heart break.

"No," Mary said, her voice barely carrying over the wind.

"No," Van Clare echoed.

"I believe in the Everything because it is real," Mary said softly. Her voice echoed Van Clare's, as if it came from a place very deep and far away.

"I believe in the Everything because it is free," Van Clare said, her voice carrying a little more conviction.

"I believe in the Everything because it would never take any person or place by force, without permission," Mary shouted, throwing out her arms wide.

"I believe in the Everything because I see it now! I see it now! I see it now! In Bonnie Judde!" Van Clare practically screamed the words out. She and Mary then began to laugh. From their middle sections and with so much conviction, their laughter carried the power scent all in itself. The world swirled around Mary as she not only smelled but felt all the best things. Bobble and Mikeala's games of tag. That smile on her father's face when Mary succeeded. The look of the sun over the water in late summer evenings when she and Katie rode their bikes so far that they were not able to breathe anymore. They stood, feet firmly planted on the ground, watching as the colors changed from blue to pink to purple to golden-gray.

The air around them shifted and sang. Bonnie Judde lifted his hands again and a ball of golden light formed on each palm. The bronze cloud shrank back from him as the air vibrated and the insults it hurled at him turned more and more useless. The ball of golden light reached his elbows. Bonnie Judde raised his arms above his head and threw the golden light straight into the center of the bronze cloud. The explosion was so intense that Mary had to grapple to keep her seat and Van Clare landed with a thud behind her on WindRunner's back. She had not stopped laughing.

The air rained golden around them, and Bonnie Judde turned his exhausted but glowing face towards them. WindRunner let out a caw of joy as Bonnie Judde and LightningChaser flew back to them. They stopped a wingspan away so that they did not need to Mindspan to talk.

"I'm so sorry, Oracle Judde," Van Clare said, with an intensity Mary had never seen before. "I didn't mean… I mean, what happened? What was that?"

"That was worse than anything we have feared," Bonnie Judde said. "That was the Everything turned inside out."

"There's more," Mary said, quietly. "I saw, I saw the inside of the camp. I need to tell you. I just—I just, I don't know how."

"Then we have to hurry," Van Clare said, quickly, already sitting and attaching her leg restraints. As she spoke across the Mindspan to tell WindRunner to fly, LightningChaser and Bonnie Judde were already gone, sprinting back towards Luminos over the mountains.

CHAPTER ELEVEN

Mary's eye were drooping with exhaustion. WindRunner was exhausted and Mary could not tell whether she was the one that was tired, or if she were feeling the Thunderbird's fatigue. She was sure it was a combination of both. Van Clare was silent. If she were thinking about their encounter with whatever that brownish coppery-colored thing was, the Thunderbird Captain did not want to talk about it. WindRunner flapped his great wings and pushed them onward. The air grew dimmer around them, and Mary knew that the sun would set soon. The flight back to Luminos was long.

The clouds thinned out after they flew over the Mountains. Mary blinked behind her goggles and wished that she could rub her eyes. She had to tell the rest of the Resistors what happened over the Shoeboxian camp, but she was not sure that she would be able to. Images, thoughts, and smells all jumbled together in her mind and tumbled over each other like rocks in a rock tumbler.

In the distance, a bright star settled on the horizon, a tiny dot at the edge of the rolling hills beneath them. Mary focused on the spot and after several more minutes of flying, she realized it was not a star, but Luminos glowing like a beacon. As the dusk settled around WindRunner's wings, the City glowed brighter, as if its walls were collecting the last of the light from the setting sun. Mary remembered that Flores had said they glowed blue at night. From this distance, Luminos looked like a circular cake that someone had set three large, fused cylinders in the middle of for decoration.

Outside the City, Mary could see various camps and buildings laid out around the base of its walls. One of those must have been the Barns for Flycycle repairs that Cody mentioned that day. Mary wondered where the refugees from other cities lived. Maybe they were all in the outermost ring, like she had seen earlier.

She could see Bonnie Judde and LightningChaser now, not too far ahead of them. LightningChaser had to be tired too, especially with Bonnie Judde standing on his back like that. Mary felt WindRunner laugh through their bond. The other Thunderbird and its rider became shadowy and dark, as the walls of Luminos began to glow against the fading light.

We're not going to land at the public Circles, Van Clare's voice crackled over the Mindspan. Mary wanted to turn around, as it sounded like the Thunderbird Captain might have been crying. Based on the discovery of her new power, wouldn't Mary have smelled it? All of this was very confusing. Van Clare continued, *Lady Kathryn says to fly all the way up to the left tower and we'll get off there.*

Heard and received, WindRunner said, the pain of exhaustion in his voice. Mary sent calming thoughts of strength down their newly forged bond. She felt the Thunderbird's gratitude in response.

They were close to flying over the public landing circles now. From this height, Mary could see four different sets of landing circles, each branching from four different entrances to the City, like spokes on a wheel. Mary wondered where the four different roads led to, and to what other parts of LeeChee she might be able to travel. The City stretched beneath them. People moved around the rings in little dots of activity, casting shadows against the glowing light of the walls. Mary decided then that Luminos was the most beautiful place she had ever seen.

WindRunner swooped towards the left tower and glided up to its top. People stood on the circle, waiting for them to land. WindRunner glided above them as they watched LightningChaser touch down and land. WindRunner then cut two more circles through the sky, losing altitude on each one and landed with all four clawed feet on one of the black quarters of the landing circle. The great Thunderbird shook out his wings, as Mary and Van Clare slid off his back. Mary's legs were tired and sore and she stumbled a little bit as she made her way around WindRunner until she could look him in his great, golden eyes. She didn't say anything but wrapped her arms around his neck.

"I'm all right, warrior," he said softly, his beak clicking over her shoulder. She stepped back, and saw a smile around the tiredness in his eyes.

"You have fought well, and bravely," Lady Kathryn's voice said from behind Mary. Mary turned to find a group of adults and Teeny and Corb staring at her. Lady Kathryn continued. "WindRunner, you have been of great service to us today. Do you wish to remain and speak with us, or do you need to return to your own People and make a report?"

"I should go," WindRunner said, his voice rumbling. "I will take some food and water here with LightningChaser and then we should fly to the Screes. The Lumon will want to know what has happened."

LightningChaser was on the other side of the landing circle, but clicked her beak in agreement or frustration, Mary couldn't tell. WindRunner lifted his wings and glided over to the other Thunderbird. Loey Cody jogged behind him. He stopped to have a word with the two Thunderbirds, as two People in rider uniforms turned on a giant spigot to release water for the exhausted creatures.

Mary turned around again. Several sets of eyes stared at her. Lady Kathryn, Bonnie Judde, Flores,

Teeny, and Corb all stood in a line, Teeny nervously stepped from one foot to the other. Next to them stood two men that Mary had not yet met. One was tall and so thin that his giant blue eyes bugged out of the pale white skin of his face. He looked skeletal and old. Next to him stood another old man of average height who had dark black hair and eyes, and a nose that was too large for his otherwise handsome brown face. They both wore sweeping green robes that were slashed with multicolored fabric from shoulder to hip. Mary did notice that they had fewer colors than Rickface.

"Mary Jingo of the Shadowlands meet my dads," Van Clare said, appearing at Mary's right elbow. "This is Forecaster E.B. Father and Oracle Heavy Dill."

"Hello," Mary said, as the tall, thin man that Van Clare had identified as the Father stepped forward.

"Let me see you, Mary Jingo. I hear that you already have abilities, great abilities. You were able to sniff out the Shoeboxians, weren't you? I bet they stink," the old man said with a laugh.

"Give her some space, Eric," the other man named Heavy Dill said. He smiled down at Mary with a knowing kindness that helped her relax slightly.

Loey Cody had jogged back over to where their party was gathered.

"We should go inside," the Aerial Commander said. "I fear we have a lot to discuss and most of it is not good news."

They entered the tower through a wide set of wooden double doors, one of the few things Mary had seen in the tower that was not gray or white. They walked along a circular hall, passing only flikers and Thunderbird riders through this part of the tower. Loey Cody walked several steps ahead of the group, occasionally having a whispered word with Thunderbird and Flike Captains as they passed.

"Yes, yes," the Father said, after Mary was silent for a few moments. "We need to hear what you saw, Mary Jingo. Or, in your case, smelled, if you do not mind telling us."

"I don't even understand what I smelled or saw today," Mary said to the old man. Something about his presence made her feel brave enough to speak. "It doesn't make any sense."

"We believe in you, Mary!" Teeny said, walking next to Mary.

Mary and the rest of the group entered a giant round room. At intervals around the walls were floor to ceiling windows made of multicolored glass. Each one was locked shut, but Mary could see how they could be thrown open to allow a Thunderbird or Flike to fly inside. A rail ran around the edge of the great domed ceiling above that was clearly a Thunderbird perch.

The entire room was a gleaming grayish-white, with giant round tiles going from one wall to the other. The walls themselves were pristine and smooth, as if the inside of a mountain had been hewn out. Long benches and rectangular tables were pushed against the wall. In the center of the gray-white tiled floor, a huge round table was laden with all kinds of food. Mary eyed the table with a rumbling in her stomach.

Large orbs of light floated around the room at random, giving the white and gray surfaces a golden glow. They were larger versions of the orbs that Mikeala had summoned on their days of walking through the hills and after Mary's first fight with the Shoeboxians. It felt like all of that had happened months and years ago.

"During festivals," Van Clare said, as she came to stand next to Mary, "oracles like our Teeny and Corb will spend many hours transforming this blank space into whatever they can dream up. I'm sad you won't get to see it that way tonight."

Mary nodded, having no response to what that would even look like. The room was beautiful without any Everything-made flowers or vines. What would it be like with the tapestries of flowers and leaves like she had seen Corb make that morning?

"I can't do this, Van Clare. I can't speak to all of these People. I'm so afraid."

"I know, Mary. I am honestly still so shaken by what we saw. We haven't even had a chance to talk about it."

"Something else, Van Clare," Mary said quietly. They moved to the table and Van Clare began to heap a small plate with food. "WindRunner swore to protect me, and now, I can feel him… in my mind."

The Thunderbird Captain stopped and put the plate down. She turned and looked at Mary, her face unreadable.

"He swore an oath you?" Van Clare said slowly.

"I guess so?" Mary said, with the creeping sensation in her stomach that she had done something wrong.

Van Clare opened her mouth to respond, when a loud clap resounded and the large plates of food on the table disappeared. Large chairs now sat around the table. Van Clare picked up her plate, moved a few seats down and sat. Mary caught a faint smell of something fiery and peppery off of the Thunderbird Captain. Was Van Clare jealous?

"Okay, sit down everyone," Loey Cody said. He motioned around the table for People to take seats. "Teeny and Corb, usually you would not be invited to a council such as this due to your age and lack of training, but we may need your assistance."

Corb sat up straighter in her chair. Teeny leaned back and not so subtly rolled her eyes. Just then, from the hallway, Mary could hear three familiar voices, arguing at a great volume.

"I am well enough, I am! Mikeala let me go!" Bobble appeared in the doorway, looking smaller than ever in such a big, open room. Mikeala and then Rickface were hot on his heels, as the three keepers made an extremely noisy entrance into the room. Mary was sure that she heard Bonnie Judde utter a small huff.

"Really, Cody," Bonnie Judde said, crossing his thin arms across his chest. "We don't have time for this."

Rickface snapped his fingers over his shoulder and the huge double doors to the room closed shut.

"You will need us, Oracle Judde. In the end. You will need us," Rickface said, casting a look so powerful at Bonnie Judde that Mary felt for the first time how formidable the keeper could be. Mikeala appeared at Mary's elbow and pushed a plate of snacks in front of her with a wink. She then rejoined Bobble.

"You all are terrible hosts, not even ensuring that our guest gets to eat before giving a report. Besides, it looks like seats are available," Mikeala said, as she and Bobble took two chairs next to each other that were the perfect size to accommodate the keepers' smaller heights.

"Thank you for coming," Loey Cody said to the three keepers, and then cast a silencing look at Bonnie Judde. They were all seated now. Loey Cody looked around from Lady Kathryn, to Flores, to Teeny and Corb, Van Clare, Bonnie Judde, the Father, Heavy Dill, Bobble, Mikeala, Rickface, and then his eyes settled on Mary.

"We need a full report. Van Clare informed us via Mindspan that you found the Shoeboxian camp and that you were attacked. Van Clare, you go first. Tell us everything."

Van Clare stood up then and gave her report. She explained how far they had flown over the mountains, where they had seen the Shoeboxians and how many she thought they numbered. She let Bonnie Judde take over then. He filled in his own details of finding the Shoeboxian camp and then began to recount their encounter with the coppery substance that was like the Everything, but was not the Everything. Mary felt a pit in the bottom of her stomach, like she needed to speak. She felt terrified but knew she had information that they would want to hear.

"Excuse me, Mr. Bonnie Judde, sir," she said quietly, surprised at how far away her own voice sounded. The oracle's head snapped towards her with a fire in his eyes that told her that he did not like to be interrupted.

"Yes?" he said sharply, his slicked back hair falling slightly out of place.

"When we were in the air, above the camp. I, could, well, I could *see* things," Mary said, trying to put words to the experience.

"Yes, all five of us could see things," Bonnie Judde replied.

"No, yes, no—I know," Mary continued. Teeny sat to her left and was looking at Mary with a face of encouragement. It gave Mary courage. "I could actually *see* Mellie. Like I was sitting right beside her. I heard her talking. It was very confusing and weird."

The group around the table fell silent. The Father tented his fingers and stared at Mary over the top of them.

"It is possible," the old man said, looking at Mary with sparkling eyes, "that the Everything allowed you to *see*, Mary Jingo. Can you explain the experience more?"

"Yes," Lady Kathryn said. "I would like to hear more."

"Well, Van Clare told me to focus and breathe and to try to smell the Shoeboxians. I did that and it worked," Mary said, looking over at her friend who gave her a small half smile. "But then, the more I smelled the Shoeboxians and Mellie, the more I felt like I was with them. And then I started to see images, hear their conversations. It was very weird. I can't—I can't really describe it."

"She could show us," Mikeala said, her black, curly hair in a myriad of small braids.

"I can?" Mary said.

"That is a very rare skill," Bonnie Judde said, shaking his head. "One that no oracle or forecaster has possessed in two hundred years."

"Earlier," Corb said softly, her brown hair falling into her face, "when we first met Mary, she showed us something briefly. A snap of a friend from her home. I didn't think anything of it—"

"Corb, you're right!" Teeny said excitedly. "She did! It was so quick, I just thought it was a strange Shadowland power."

"I say it's worth a try," Flores piped in. She had her booted feet propped up on the table. "Although, I don't know anything about how your channeling and controlling works."

"We will have to build a web, a bridge, to bring everyone in," the Father said slowly. Bonnie Judde looked very wary. "It will force us to draw on a powerful lot of the Everything and it may exhaust every single one of us, but we can try.

"You will have to be brave, Mary Jingo. When I call your name, you will need to put yourself back into the memory and force it into the web," the old man finished. He started at Mary until she nodded, even though she had no idea what that meant. He then looked at Corb and Teeny. "You two will need to work the web like we did in class two weeks ago. Build your own net and then cast it to connect with mine and Lady Kathryn's. Do you understand?"

"Wait," Lady Kathryn said, as the two young O.I.T.s nodded. Lady Kathryn pushed back from the table and stood up. "Eric, are you sure? This is a dangerous amount of the Everything to try to control."

"I cannot help you either," Heavy Dill said quietly. "I am not powerful enough to build a web of that size."

"We'll help stabilize," Rickface said. "Although Bobble will not be able to help. He is still recovering. I can bring in Cody and Van Clare as well."

Bobble folded his arms across his chest and pushed the brim of his hat low over his eyes. They all looked at each other as if they were unsure.

"Don't worry, I'll bring you in," Mikeala said, laying a hand on Bobble's arm. "You all can do this. I know that you can."

"Let us begin," the Father said.

Lady Kathryn, the Father, Bonnie Judde, Teeny and Corb began moving their hands in a complex set of swirling gestures. As they did, golden light shot from their palms and began to glow. The light became a golden thread. As their hands began to work through the air, Mary saw why they described it as a web. Each of them wove a pattern in front of them. The patterns became bigger and bigger, and Mary saw sweat standing out on the Father's brow. The edges of each of their webs began to touch and as they connected, Mary heard the Father call for the rest of the group to take hold of the edges. Van Clare grasped the glowing golden threads and her face shone brightly.

The web grew closer to Mary and it made her smile. She liked this web very much and she felt it calling to her, welcoming her to have purpose and to breathe deeply. She remembered what the Father had told her about showing all of them her memory, and how it had scared her. Now that this glowing, golden web was close, it seemed like the easiest thing in the world. She faintly heard Lady Kathryn cry that they were all connected, so Mary put her hand out and plucked a string.

CITY OF LIGHTS

Mary could see Mellie now, just as she had earlier that day. Mellie's scent had transported Mary into her tent, as if the connection of the scent memory were a bridge. Mellie was in the center of an opulent tent—complete with skins all over the floor—scratching her scarred nose and studying a giant map. She was muttering to herself about the mountains and being surrounded by a group of giant Shoeboxians.

"Look at this, Edgar," she cackled, holding up a handful of a coppery-looking substance. She shoved it towards the Shoeboxian closest to her. *"Should we make a name for it? Or maybe make it a laurel wreath. Give it a meaning. It's a victory."*

"Shut up," the Shoeboxian named Edgar said. His voice was low, gravelly and awful. Mary waited for him to spit out a rock as he spoke. He didn't look at Mellie and turned away. She stuck her tongue out at his back.

"You're only fun sometimes. Did you know that? If they would just let me blow more things up, I wouldn't have to sit here all the time with nothing to do," she frowned and pouted horribly. The scars on her face wrinkled up in an awkward mixture of delight and disgust.

"Mellie, I told you. Once we take the Imperial City, you can blow up any building or object that catches your

wicked fancy. You can even have a few of my less important Shoeboxians for fun. But we have to get there. And since you've forgotten how to control the mountains—" Mellie cut Edgar off with a hiss.

"No one controls the mountains, you idiot! Least of all me. And don't tell me you think those tossers Rickface or Bobble and Mikeala could do it. Because they couldn't!" The last sentence came out sullenly and wounded, like a child who'd had a toy taken away.

"Nothing else can keep those rabid Resistors from pursuing us," another one of the Shoeboxians said. *"We need them trapped on that side of the mountains."*

"I just need to try a little harder," Mellie said.

"You'll kill yourself," the first Shoeboxian named Edgar said.

"You'd like that," Mellie replied.

Mellie smiled cruelly at the rest of the Shoeboxians around the table. The images blurred for a moment as Mary felt a wave of fear drench her. She tried to focus—focus on the evil smell of Mellie. Mellie again came into view, standing just outside the tent with a hideous smile of glee on her face.

"Sweet, sweet, Captain Van Clare! She'll never see this one coming," Mellie cackled as she ran her hands

around the coppery substance and whispered words that Mary could not make out, and knew that she didn't want to.

Mary's vision sped back to her memory of flying on WindRunner's back and the firefight that had ensued as a scream escaped from her mouth. She saw it all over again. Bonnie Judde confronting the great copper cloud as it spewed anger and hatred towards him. She heard Van Clare jeering and laughing. She then saw Bonnie Judde burst into golden light and turn the tide. And then, as quickly as it all started, the vision was gone.

CHAPTER

TWELVE

As soon as the web broke and the vision ended, Loey Cody stood up and quietly said that he would like for Teeny, Corb, and Mary to leave the room. His eyes were fierce and terrified as he looked from Lady Kathryn to Bonnie Judde to the Father, who all sat dazed and blinking in their chairs. Teeny was not fully awake, and even Mary felt shaken and unsteady. No one responded to his request.

"What happened?" Mary asked quietly. Van Clare was pale and wan, as if she had seen a ghost.

"This is worse than we thought," Loey Cody exclaimed, jumping from his seat and putting a finger to his temple, atop his multicolored bandana. He stopped for a moment as if he were sending a message. "I have to find the Lumon. We have to go, tonight. They are going to try and trap us here so that Mellie can finally put the Imperial City under Thrall."

"Slow down, my love," Lady Kathryn said, quietly, as she seemed to still be feeling the aftereffects of her efforts. "We need to discuss this. Mellie's words were unclear. You cannot just rush into battle—"

"She has that thing! She has the Void under her control!" Loey Cody said, looking at the old man across the table. "She has turned the Everything inside out. Mary Jingo, I apologize. I would have never sent you on that mission if I had known how dangerous it would be."

"The Void?" Mary said. "Is that what attacked us in the sky?"

"Yes," Bonnie Judde said quietly. "I must warn the Emperor. He must be ready for an attack."

"Lady Kathryn is right," Heavy Dill said. "We must talk this over, send word to the Imperial City, and have a council. Mellie is a liar. This could be a trick."

"You saw it with your own eyes, Dill," Flores said softly. "This isn't a trick."

"I want the children out of the room and somewhere safe," Loey Cody said. "That's not a request. It's an order."

"Those were Mary Jingo's memories," Van Clare said defiantly. "You cannot just order her to leave now."

"No, no. Cody is right," Heavy Dill said finally, as he looked first to Loey Cody, then to the Father and then back across the table at Mary. "I will take the O.I.T.s to the study where they can rest and have a small break. We will wait for your word, Commander.

"O.I.T. Corb, O.I.T. Teeny, O.I.T. Mary Jingo, please come with me," Heavy Dill said. He gracefully stood up from his chair, his robes swishing around him.

He led the three of them out of the room. Mary felt overwhelmed that she had been referred to as O.I.T. Mary Jingo. She also felt so tired she wondered if she could make this walk to wherever they were going. Her feet dragged along the cold, white floor. She had no idea how long they walked or how many flights of stairs they descended when Teeny tiredly took a left off of the main corridor and climbed a set of ten stairs. She opened a door to a giant, round room. Unlike so many of the other rooms of Luminos, this room was warm, welcoming, and full of color. Shelves and stacks of books surrounded Mary as she made her way through the door. The rounded walls were punctuated by giant stained-glass windows and a fireplace crackled in the bend of the far wall. All around were chalk boards and chemistry sets, and anything else she could imagine in a giant room for learning. Mary drifted towards the fireplace, and the three large, overstuffed chairs and small sofa settled in front of it. Mary laid down on the sofa as Teeny and Corb each collapsed into one of the comfy chairs. All three of the O.I.T.s promptly fell asleep.

Mary awoke sometime later to a sticky, sweet smell of herbs and spices. Her eyes fluttered open. Corb was sitting up in her chair, sipping from a teacup and reading a book, with a blanket tucked around her legs. Teeny was curled in her chair, still fast asleep. Mary found that someone had draped a warm, fuzzy blanket over her while she slept. On a table in front of her sat a tea set of black porcelain, which was where the smell of herbs and spices radiated from.

Corb put a thin finger to her mouth and looked towards Teeny. She whispered: "You've both been out for a long time. Drink some tea. Oracle Dill made it. It'll help you feel better."

Mary felt like her head was full of cotton balls. She sat up on the couch, stretched and rubbed her eyes. She poured herself a cup of tea. The smell of it was so strong that Mary could tell that this tea had been made with the power of the Everything. She sipped it gently, as it was still very hot. She felt instantly better. She and Corb sat staring at the fire and sipping their tea quietly for a few minutes.

Mary felt a pressure on the outside of her mind, as if someone were knocking on the door, asking to be let in. She gently pressed back, as she asked *Who is it?*

It's Oracle Heavy Dill, was the soft reply. Mary opened the door and allowed Heavy Dill to speak with her.

I'm across the room, Mary Jingo. If you feel well enough, can you please come over here and join me?

Mary looked over her shoulder and saw Heavy Dill across the giant room, standing over one of the tables. He saw her looking and waved at her. Mary extracted herself from the couch, which was very comfy, and made her way over. Golden instruments whirred and purred on tables crammed with books. She carried her tea carefully in her hands, trying not to spill any of it on the floor.

"How do you feel, Mary Jingo?" Heavy Dill asked. He was behind a table full of gadgets and instruments, some of them giving off a heavy smell of the Everything. His robes swished pleasantly as he walked back and forth.

"I think I'm okay. I feel, well, more or less normal. Showing everyone my memories really tired me out."

Mary looked around at all the objects and instruments and wondered if she would get in trouble if she picked any of them up. She couldn't try anyway, with her hands full of a hot teacup, which she remembered and slowly sipped.

"That was a powerful bit of controlling. Not many oracles or forecasters have that talent."

Heavy Dill paused as if she were meant to respond. Mary only nodded silently.

"It seems to me that you have heard that phrase many, many times since you arrived here."

Mary thought about all the things that she had done and been able to do since she arrived in LeeChee. She had disabled Flikes in the air, called a forest to her aid, sensed an entire army of Shoeboxians, and now shown People her memories. She was in awe of it all and still unsure what any of it meant. She looked up and Heavy Dill's wise eyes were trained on her. She expected him to respond to her thoughts, as so many People here seemed to always know exactly what she was thinking.

"You have gotten better," he said.

"Better at what?"

"Better at shielding your thoughts."

"How do you know?"

"Because you were silent for a very long time, and the only thing that came across Mindspan was your wondering if I could hear your thoughts. So, either you spent that entire pause with nothing on your mind, or you have already figured out a way to quiet your mind."

Mary felt shocked. This was yet another skill that she had just developed out of the blue. The oracle began moving instruments around the table, clearing a space.

"Ancient Leechian scholars have tried to study your world for generations, Mary Jingo. We have never understood the connection between there and here, but one does exist. The problem is, anyone who has travelled between here and there, they generally do not come back. Or, if they do return, they are so confused and forgetful, they cannot account for much."

Heavy Dill paused here, as if waiting for Mary to respond or ask a question. When she did not, ever the good teacher, he continued on.

"Some of the most archaic texts call LeeChee a 'Borderland.' It has only been in the last 100 annuals that scholars began to call your world the Shadowlands, as if it were a shadow of our world. But to very frank, I don't know if this world is a shadow of your world or if the opposite is true.

"When towns started to fall under Thrall some annuals ago, we oracles, forecasters, and keepers banded together. We were going to find a cure for the evil, an end to the threat. Nothing worked. Nothing. Hours of research, search parties, collections, samples—it feels like every person in this tower has been working towards an answer. But our land has continued to list, becoming dark and brown and empty. Until, well, you."

"I don't understand," Mary said quietly, setting her empty teacup on the table. "How am I the cure?"

Heavy Dill's deep brown eyes softened in his face, as he looked at Mary with a deep tenderness.

"Oh, Mary Jingo. The burden of youth is so heavy; always underestimated, but also often aware and often right about the truth of what you see. You are the cure because you have brought us something most important. Something that we, the mighty Resistors, had lost sight of. You have brought us hope and reminded us of what the Everything is, and does, and can be."

Mary thought about this for a long moment. She reached to the table and touched a set of golden scales, sending them tilting back and forth. They were cool to her fingertips and alive, tinkling as she touched them as if they laughed merrily. She was a reminder. Suddenly, and ever so softly, a few of the puzzle pieces that Mary had been working through in her mind snapped into place.

"I'm not the cure," she said softly, watching the scales tilt back and forth. "I don't understand why I can do any of the things I have done. But I am happy to help you. I really like it here."

"And I am happy to help you and teach you in any way that I can," Heavy Dill said, as he chuckled softly to himself. Mary smelled something light and airy on him like peppermint. He was impressed with her.

He had cleared a large space on the table in front of him. A circular object draped in canvas sat in front of him. He beckoned for her to come around the table and stand next to him.

"Earlier, when I was droning on and on about the connection between your world and ours, did you think I was just playing the boring old professor?" Heavy Dill asked and smiled at the look on Mary's face.

"No, I mean, a little. But I thought it was interesting."

"It was because of this," Heavy Dill said. He gestured towards the canvas-draped object. "Rickface, the Father, and I have long thought that the loss of the Everything and the rise of the Void is due to some connection between your world and ours."

"Bobble and Mikeala mentioned that."

"Aw, yes, they are wise keepers. And you are a good listener. This object allows us to see into the Shadowlands for very, very short amounts of time— about forty-five seconds before it will shut off and need to recharge. We have been using it to try and gauge the state of things in your world. And by the look of them, it is not so good."

Mary didn't quite understand this. In her quiet neighborhood, at her school—her life was okay. She rode her bike and had Katie. Sure, some of the other kids at school weren't necessarily nice to her, but otherwise, most of it seemed normal.

"I'm not sure what you mean," she said, looking down at her sandalled feet.

"It's okay if you don't quite understand. That can be a longer conversation for a different time. What you will do now is use this object to have a conversation with your parents."

CHAPTER
THIRTEEN

Hannie and Harold Jingo sat on their living room sofa. Hannie held a small three inch by three inch square mirror with a simple gold frame in her hand. The strange-looking little man who had woken them up out of their bed six nights ago had said their daughter would make contact with them. It was part of their agreement. It was the only part of their agreement that had kept Hannie from throttling the little man named Rickface against a wall. That and the images he had been able to conjure in the small mirror of Mary walking safely through a field, smiling up at a blonde teenager with a mohawk.

"You can use this mirror whenever you like," Rickface told them. He stood on their coffee table and was at eye level with the Jingos who sat on the couch. He had just spent several minutes explaining his world 'LeeChee,' 'the Everything' and Mary's roll in all of it. Hannie felt her mind spin like a top as the small man continued to speak about the mirror. "It operates on intention and the Everything, and is very simply designed so that even you Shadowlanders can use it. All you need to do is look at it and focus on your daughter and she will appear."

Hannie had instantly put the mirror into her cupped palms and focused on Mary with all of her mind and heart. Nothing happened.

"It's not working!" she said, a tremble of fear in her voice.

"My apologies," Rickface had continued, clasping his hands behind his back. "When I said, 'whenever you like,' I meant that it would only work once a day and only for few moments. The Everything is shrinking in LeeChee and is near non-existent here in the Shadowlands."

"I don't understand the words that you are using, sir," Harold had said then. His dark brown eyes narrowed with fear. "But what I do know is that you have kidnapped our daughter. I am going to call the police."

"I didn't kidnap her," Rickface replied. "She wanted to go. I gave her a choice and she decided on her own accord what she wanted to do."

"She is a CHILD."

"She is a child. A very important child. More important than either of you know or understand. We have sent beacons for weeks and months, looking for a person who understands the Everything. Your daughter was the first to even see them for what they are!"

"You are not making any sense. Bring her back or I will have you arrested!"

"You have no idea the things that are at stake here!" Rickface almost screeched. He pulled on his hair, his irregular features jumping and twitching on his strangely shaped face. "How long will I have to explain this to you? It's not just my world, it's your world too. If the Everything is destroyed, your world will suffer, just as ours has. Why can you not see it? I will make you an oath. I will swear to you on the Everything and it will be a binding contract.

And if I fail your daughter, then I will pay the price with my own life. I will swear it to you."

"I don't care about your world or your 'magical' oath! I care about my daughter and her safety! We don't know you. You could be lying to us. You could be holding her for ransom somewhere. Do you have any idea what you are asking?"

"Wait, Harold, no," Hannie said quietly, looking down at the mirror in her hands. Tears had formed in the corners of her husband's eyes as he looked at her with shock. "Strange things have happened. I haven't heard from Sue Collins in over three weeks."

"That's right," Harold said. "You haven't."

"It seems like more and more of our friends are off on wild, lavish vacations, all over the world, but we can't get in touch with them. None of them answer their phones. Don't you think it's strange?"

The two men stared at her in silence. She felt a deep sense of calm, as if all of her best memories surrounded her and enfolded her in their arms. She felt a peace so deep that she had surprised herself with her next words.

"I love Mary more than anything and want to protect her more than anything. In one sense, I ask myself what kind of mother am I if I let my daughter do this? But, on the other hand, what kind of mother am I if I don't let her go? Let my strong, capable girl try?"

"How do we know she will be safe?" Harold pleaded with his wife.

"We don't. But she went to summer camp last year and did zip lines and mountain hikes and mud pits and she came back all right. I can't explain it, Harry. I just, I just feel like this is something that we need to let her do. Whatever it means. I want to accept Rickface's oath. We will believe you if you swear."

Harold had stared at her for a very long and uncomfortable moment. She watched the wheels turn in his brain through the concentration in his eyes.

"I don't like this. I don't like it at all. But I trust you, Han. If you feel like we should trust Rickface, then I will. BUT—if anything happens to our daughter, if there is a scratch on her, I will personally see to it that you NEVER get out of prison, in your world or ours."

"The oath will ensure that, if I fail her," Rickface replied, gravely. He closed his eyes. "I swear to you Hannie and Harold Jingo, I swear on the Everything that I will do all that is in my power to protect your daughter, Mary Jingo, and if I fail her, my own life shall be forfeit."

As he finished, a jet of golden light shot from Rickface's right hand and split into two strands. It looped around the right wrists of Harold and Hannie for a few seconds, glowing and moving in the dim light of their living room. It had felt hot and cold at the same time. When it disappeared, Hannie still felt a tingling sensation on her wrist. She could see the faintest golden shimmer in the dim light, as if she wore a bracelet that she could hardly see.

"We are bound," Rickface said solemnly and nodded his head, as if thinking to himself. "As long as that mark on your wrist remains, Mary is safe and whole. I will see to it that she contacts you soon."

"She will be able to contact us? Can we speak to her?" Harold asked, running his thumb and forefinger around his wrist.

"The mirror, of course. Once I am able, I will have Mary contact you using a similar device. The connection will be brief, but I will make an assumption that she will want to speak with you as well. The mirror will begin to blink and glow golden when she is about to make contact. I would keep it near you at all times."

With that, the little man had snapped his fingers and disappeared in a puff of golden glitter that lingered in their living room for several hours after he had gone. Hannie had kept the mirror near her every moment for the past six days. Even during work, she kept it nearby on her desk at the hospital. At night, they slept with it between them in their bed, on the pillow, so that the glow would wake them if Mary were to call. Contact? Try to reach them?

Every morning, she and Harold would crowd around it, and think about their daughter. Images of her would flash in front of them. A few of them did not frighten either of them at all. Mary sleeping peacefully in a large bed, walking through a field with a woman the size of Rickface, and an image of her smiling as a city teemed around her. Other images disturbed them slightly, and made them clutch their wrists and talk about the possibility of Mary being in danger. These included Mary with golden goggles over her eyes, flying through the air.

In spite of themselves, and watching through their tiny window of a mirror, the Jingos knew what

Rickface had said was true. Mary had done and would do amazing things. They were right to let her try.

Five minutes ago, during dinner, the mirror on the table had begun to blink and glow gold. Hannie and Harold rushed to pick it up and now sat on their sofa, waiting for their daughter to appear. Sam lingered nearby, as nervous for his sister's wellbeing as his parents were, even if he didn't want to say so.

The mirror began to glow again, sparkling against the lamp light in their living room. The glow began to swirl then suddenly, the face of their daughter, Mary Jingo, appeared. The four of them (Sam included) burst into tears.

Mary sat down exactly where Heavy Dill instructed. The chair was cushioned, but not quite comfortable. She felt nervous and excited. She had no idea how she would talk to her parents, but this was LeeChee. She never knew what would happen next.

"I'm going to remove this cover," Heavy Dill said, as he placed his hand on the heavy piece of canvas. "Once I lift it, focus your mind on your home, your mother, and your father, and your brother. They have a similar device that will connect to this one and you will be able to speak with them. The connection will only last for a few minutes."

"Is it a cell phone? For FaceTime?" Mary asked.

"What do you mean? What is a cell phone?"

"It's a, uh, well, it's a box that you can use to call someone, and you know—speak to them."

"No, Mary Jingo, I've never heard of such a thing," Heavy Dill said, holding his head to the side with a grin. "This is a mirror. Your parents have one similar. You have to focus."

"Okay," Mary replied. She couldn't think of anything else to say.

Heavy Dill placed his hand on the cover and gently removed it. He revealed a round mirror about the size of a large pepperoni pizza, sitting on a stand. It had a simple brown wood frame. Mary stared at her reflection for several seconds. She looked up at the oracle for guidance. He simply opened his hand as if to say, 'you know what to do.'

Mary took a deep breath and closed her eyes. She focused on her mother and father and Sam. She thought about how much she loved them. How much she missed them. When she opened her eyes, her father and mother's faces were pressed close together staring at the glass. As realization spread across their faces, Mary smiled and laughed. Her mother and father began to laugh too, and then they both began to speak at once.

"MARY!" her mother said, her voice full of concern. "Are you okay? Are you hurt? You don't look hurt."

"You look okay, firefly," her father said. "Why did you leave? How did you get out of the house without us noticing?"

Suddenly, the picture shook as Sam pushed his way between his parents. Mary saw a brief flash of the ceiling. When Mary saw the three of them again, Sam was wedged between her parents, the three of them hardly able to fit in frame.

"Hi Mary," Sam said sheepishly, his eyes were red as if he had been crying too. "Glad you're okay."

"I am okay," Mary said, wiping the tears from her eyes. "I really am. It's been a crazy couple of days. But I am okay. I miss you."

"We miss you too," her mother exclaimed. "Are you sure you're all right? You left so suddenly. I've been worried sick."

"I am. I really am," Mary said, as she surprised herself with how okay she actually was. "I'm sorry I just left. Rickface said that they needed help and he showed me the Everything, and I just, I don't know. It felt like the right thing to do."

Mary's mother's eyes softened. Her dad looked at her with a mixture of fear and pride. Sam looked like he might try to hug the mirror. Mary felt like she was going to cry all over again.

"Don't apologize, Mary. We aren't angry. We just want you to be safe," her mother said.

"Are they taking good care of you?" her father asked.

"Sure," Mary replied. "I've learned all kinds of things since I've been here. They're even going to let me be an Oracle in Training, so I'm learning how to channel and control, even though I don't really know what any of it means. Oh! And I flew on the back of a Thunderbird. And we got attacked once. Well, twice, I guess, if you count the forest and in the sky earlier. And my new friend Corb came into my room and made flowers appear everywhere. And more stuff too…"

Mary trailed off as her mother's eyes became wider and wider with every word she spoke.

"But I really am okay. Tons of adults are around and they never let me do this stuff alone. I promise."

"What's a Thunderbird, Mary?" Sam asked. "And are you really getting to fly? That's so cool! What does it feel like? Did you want to throw up? I bet if I flew I would definitely throw up."

Mary's parents looked at each other over Sam's head as Mary smiled at her brother.

"It's been so cool, Sam. And I don't know, a little scary? But still really cool. I can't wait to show you all the stuff they have here. You would love it. These scary guys called Shoeboxians showed up and they STINK! Like worse than anything I've ever smelled."

"Whoa! Mary! Why do you get to do all the fun stuff?" Sam asked, looking disappointed in the mirror. The image began to waver and Mary remembered that Heavy Dill said the connection wouldn't last very long.

"I really am okay," Mary said again to her parents. "They are taking very good care of me, and I think I am doing something important here. It's hard to explain, but this world, I don't know. I can feel it. It needs me."

"We love you, Mary," her mother said, as the picture began to fade, tears forming in her eyes. "I can't help but feel like the worst mother for letting you do this, but we are proud of you. We want you to try."

"You're so brave, Mary. We love you," her father said.

"Bring me back something cool!" Sam said.

"I love you too," Mary said, as the mirror began to glow and her parents and Sam's faces faded away. Mary sat for several long moments, as she gazed at her own reflection and wondered if she had changed.

Corb and Mary were sitting over a round game board that Mary did not understand when Teeny finally woke up from her very long nap. The curly-haired O.I.T. sat up in her chair and stretched her arms above her head with a loud yawn. Mary looked down at the gameboard that was full of tiny porcelain frogs and bears.

"So, a bear can slide to knock over a frog, but a frog only jumps over a bear? And red circles are double jumps or slides, and blue circles mean you go back one space?"

"Yes," Corb said, nodding over the game board. "Should we play? You might understand it better once we start to play."

Teeny wandered over from the chair, a blanket wrapped around her shoulders.

"How are you both so awake? Controlling that much of the Everything made me need a nap. Also, it has to be almost midnight."

"Maybe if you paid more attention in lessons you wouldn't get so tired," Corb said with a smile on her face, staring at the game board. Teeny stuck her tongue out at her. "And it is late, but neither one of us felt like sleeping."

"You sound like Professor 'I'm so heavy I'll crush you,'" Teeny said. She looked around the room. "Speaking of—where is he?"

"He went to find the Father. Something about important Resistor business. He told us to stay here," Corb replied. "And did you think to check the room before you called him a name?"

"OOOoooo! I love Frog Bear Flunderbuss! Can I play the winner?"

"You can play now," Mary replied. "I don't know what's going on."

Teeny noisily pulled a chair across the room to sit next to Mary. The noise of the chair was so loud, Mary almost didn't hear the tapping on the glass of the nearby window. She knew instantly that it was WindRunner. She ran to the window, lifted a latch on the stained-glass frame, and opened the window. The Thunderbird's giant head was almost too big to fit through.

"Hello, Mary Jingo of the Shadowlands," he clicked his beak.

"WindRunner! Hi!"

Corb and Teeny came and stood behind Mary. They both had their heads bowed and eyes lowered to the floor. Teeny curtsied.

"Caw my caw and well met. I am Teeny, an Oracle in Training of FarFlung. I am pleased to make your acquaintance."

"Caw my caw and well met. I am Corb, an Oracle in Training of Luminos. I am pleased to make your acquaintance."

They both put their palms to their foreheads and continued to look at the floor.

"Caw my caw and well met, Oracles in Training Corb and Teeny. I am WindRunner, Thunderbird and I am pleased to make your acquaintances," the Thunderbird rumbled. "I like your friends, Mary Jingo of the Shadowlands. They are very polite."

"I guess you could say they are polite most of the time," Mary said with a wink towards Teeny. "What are you doing here?"

"The Thunderbird Corps and the Flike army are moving. Based on the intelligence you were able to provide during your meeting with Commander Cody and the other Resistors, they have deemed that the Imperial City may fall under attack. We are to go there immediately to defend it."

"Now?" Mary asked, looking at the Thunderbird's golden eyes. "You're going right now?"

"Yes, Mary Jingo. I would have told you via Mindspan, but this chamber is warded in some way. I was not able to reach you."

"Oh yes," Teeny said brightly. "The Father and Heavy Dill did that. It is supposed to protect us, but also to keep us from cheating on tests."

"Be that as it may," WindRunner continued. "Our bond prohibits me from going too far from you, Mary Jingo. I am sworn to your safety, so I have requested to stay nearby while the rest of the army leaves."

"You have?" Mary said, surprised that the Thunderbird would stay.

"No need, really," Corb said, in her most mature voice. "Luminos is one of the safest places in all of LeeChee."

"Aren't you the Lumon's son? And her heir?" Teeny asked then quickly added, "Mr. WindRunner, sir?"

"That is not of concern. I swore an oath to Mary Jingo of the Shadowlands and I intend to keep it," WindRunner said.

"Oh, WindRunner," Mary said, stepping forward and wrapping her arms around the Thunderbird's neck. "You don't have to stay to keep me safe. But if you want to, I will accept your protection."

"I will be circling the Towers and will make a post on the landing circle above. I don't like that we cannot Mindspan while you are within the wards. If you need me, you can pull the thread of our bond. I will know to come to you."

Mary nodded. She looked at the Thunderbird for a long moment.

"Should we be frightened, WindRunner? Do you really think Mellie is going to attack the Imperial City?"

"The Lumon and your Commander Cody are infinitely wise. They would not take off with the army if they were not certain that the attack would be towards the Imperial City. You truly have nothing to fear.

"It is very late, young O.I.T.s," he remarked, clicking his beak. "You should all get some sleep."

With that, WindRunner cawed lightly and pulled his head from the window. Mary shut the window behind him against the cold night air.

"What did you mean when you said he was the Lumon's son?" Mary asked Corb. Corb swept her long, dark hair over one shoulder and walked back over to the game board.

"The Lumon is the leader of all Thunderbirds. Well, all of the Thunderbirds we deal with. Wild Thunderbirds still live in the Screes on the other side of the Disappearing Mountains. All Thunderbirds, whether they are the ones you meet here, or the ones in the Screes, elect their leadership through a very complex system of checks, balances, and physical tests."

"Snooze alert, Corb! Mary Jingo doesn't care about any of that. She wants you to teach her to play Frog Bear Flunderbuss. Just like I want to play Frog Bear Flunderbuss."

Teeny ran from the window back to the game board. Mary looked over at Corb, who rolled her eyes. They had just taken their seats around the game board when they heard the door to the study open. Heavy Dill bustled his way into the room. Three sets of golden goggles hung from his left hand.

"O.I.T.s, you must go to your chambers now. It is late," the oracle said as he neared them. His rich brown eyes looked tired and weary. "Before he left, Commander Cody asked me to ward your rooms, so that is what I have done. You will need to take these googles with you. They will allow you to Mindspan with each other and with me from the warded rooms."

"Will I be able to speak to WindRunner?" Mary asked.

Heavy Dill sank heavily into a nearby chair.

"I would think so, yes. Thunderbird control of the Everything is quite different from our own. I am certain that even without the goggles, if WindRunner truly desired to reach you, he would be able to. Although, if he and his cohort get far enough away, it may become more difficult. It also depends on the strength of your oath and bond."

Mary nodded quietly. She wondered behind the shields of her mind if she should tell Heavy Dill that WindRunner was not far from them now. He had chosen to stay here with her rather than fly with his cohort. Before she could speak, Teeny piped up.

"Are you okay, professor? You look exhausted."

"Weaving the wards was much work, even with my wonderful husband's help. Plus, we had to control into these goggles to make them work properly. It was quite the task."

"We are sorry to have caused trouble," Corb said quietly.

"Trouble? What trouble? You three are the very least of my worries, good students that you are. I am tasked to help Lady Kathryn look after Luminos while the Father and all the rest run off to defend the Imperial City. If anything, that is the trouble. I was never one for rulership, I am old and only a scholar. No warrior lives in my bones," Heavy Dill said with a laugh, as he straightened in the chair and gathered himself. "You three are the future of oracles in Luminos. Your safety is very important. Even though, I doubt we'll have anything dramatic happen here tonight, Cody and Kathryn are always so quick with precautions."

"Did Van Clare go?" Mary asked, wondering about her friend and afraid for her safety. "Did she go with the army?"

"Yes, she flew out with her cohort an hour ago. She is very accomplished, my daughter. The youngest Thunderbird Captain ever, flying by the age of four years old" the oracle paused for a moment, deep in his own thoughts. And then he said to himself, "She will be fine. Yes, she will be fine."

"But enough chitter chatter. You three must be off to bed. It has been a long day and you need your rest. We have many lessons to begin and return to tomorrow."

Heavy Dill swept from his chair and beckoned the three O.I.T.s to follow him. Corb went first. She caught up to the oracle's side and began speaking with him about a new kind of channeling that she would like to attempt. Teeny went next, taking the golden goggles that were offered to her. Mary lingered for a moment next to the game board. She looked back at the mirror on a table to her left. She wanted to take it to her room and sleep beside it. It was her only link to her parents.

"Mary Jingo," Heavy Dill called from the door of the study. Mary could not see him, but she could hear his voice. "Come along now. You can use the mirror again tomorrow."

Mary was very tired of everyone listening to her thoughts. The next table over, she noticed a small device that looked exactly like the dissipators she had seen Cody and Van Clare use. She took a deep breath and imagined a wall around her mind. She hopped over to the table and grabbed it. She felt a small thrill, as she concealed it in the ball of her fist. Was this stealing? Mary had never stolen anything in her life. Her heart raced as she followed Heavy Dill, Corb, and Teeny out of the study.

Mary awoke late the next morning. She looked around the room at the honeysuckles still trailing down the walls and wondered how long it would take her to learn this skill. After asking the room for a hot shower, breakfast, and clean clothes, she put on the golden goggles and contacted Corb and Teeny. They came to her room quickly and explained that Heavy Dill had given them the day off from studies.

"So, what should we do today?" Teeny asked, as she made small, twirling circles around the room. Corb and Mary sat at the small table together. "Should we just sit and wait for the army to return? Or for Sir Heaviness to call us back into class?"

"We could show Mary the gardens on the third ring. I haven't been out there to them in a very long time."

"Oooo, the Gardens of Paradise. That could be fun," Teeny replied, twirling dramatically and flopping on Mary's bed.

"What are the Gardens of Paradise?" Mary asked.

"No one but out-of-towners call them that," Corb said, with a wave of her hand. "It's where the grower scholars perform most of their experiments. In the old days, supposedly they had an entire floor on the tower to practice, but it overgrew, so they moved them to larger part of the City."

"That sounds neat!" Mary said.

"Ugh, it's such a long walk, though," Teeny said, propping herself up on her elbow.

"I can see if WindRunner will take us!"

"Now you're talking!" Teeny said, hopping off the bed.

WindRunner agreed to the trip, as he didn't have anything else to do.

"All Thunderbirds are equipped to carry three riders, although we seldom do. But you three are so small," he said proudly, when they met him on the landing circle atop the tower. "It will be nothing for me."

Teeny and Corb greeted him just as timidly as they had the day before. He clicked his beak as they climbed on.

Mary showed Corb and Teeny where to clip their feet into the restraints and made sure they had their goggles in place, even though Teeny didn't necessarily need them.

Here we go, WindRunner said, as he launched off the platform. Teeny screamed wildly across the Mindspan.

The flight was only for a few moments, but it took Corb and Teeny several long breaths to calm down once they landed in the third ring of the City.

"That. Was. AMAZING!" Teeny screeched. Corb straightened her O.I.T. tunic and smoothed her hair.

"That's one word for it."

"Thank you, WindRunner," Mary said, as she stood in front of the great Thunderbird.

"Call me when are ready to fly home," he said, as he spread his vast wings and jumped into the air.

Mary, Corb, and Teeny walked around the curve of the ring towards a set of giant stone gates that were wide open. They were covered in all kinds of green, blue, and purple creeping vines. The smell from the garden was so strong Mary felt faint. It was alive, growing, and pulsing. She also faintly detected the smell of the Everything.

"It's just open like this all the time?" Mary asked, as they passed through the gates.

"It is," Corb said. "The growers see it as their gift to the City, and really all of LeeChee."

"They grow all of this?" Mary asked, passing all kinds of plants. Tall plants, short plants, trees, vines, and flowers, all curving around trellises or growing up stone outcroppings. Little fountains and brooks ran next to the path they walked down. It reminded her of a movie about a chocolate factory she had watched in school, though she was certain that these plants were not candy.

"They do," Teeny said. "Corb wants to be a grower. She just won't admit it."

"I haven't decided yet," Corb replied. She stopped and took a small purple flower into her hand. Her hand glowed golden for a moment, washing the three of them in the smell of all the best things in the world. The flower opened in her palm, unfurling like a sunrise. "Most of these plants won't grow anywhere else. The Everything has shrunk so much in the past two hundred annuals. It's only Luminos' ancient tie to the Everything that keeps them alive."

Teeny shrugged her shoulders. They continued walking as Corb explained that the garden had rings much like the City. The outermost was for experiments, then trees, then crops, then flowers and herbs.

"The final ring," she said, as they continued walking past what Mary thought looked a lot like corn.

"—is for the Everything," Mary finished for her, breathing in deeply. "I can smell it from here."

The smell of the Everything became stronger and stronger as they came closer to the center of the garden. The plants began to take on a golden hue.

They passed a few growers now, each in their green tunics with a lighter green slash from shoulder to hip. They waved at the O.I.T.s and commented about how nice the weather was that day. At the center of the garden, a small golden fountain glittered and tinkled in the light of about twenty different golden plants. It smelled alive and wonderful.

"How?" Mary asked.

"Oracles and forecasters used to be more common," Corb said, as she stood next to Mary and stared at the fountain with her. "One out of every three children tested had some aptitude for the Everything. Even then, the ones who couldn't channel or control could still sense it with ease. We used to have time, People, and energy to create things like this. These plants have excessive healing properties. One cutting from one of these plants can cause an entire field to sprout to life."

"Yeah, and you can also do this," Teeny said, as she conjured a golden ball of light between her hands and threw it into the air. It exploded into a million tiny sparkling stars.

"Amazing," Mary said to herself. She stood in front of a golden weeping willow, whose branches tinkled like music in the breeze. She felt the need to curtsy to it slightly and tell it hello.

Mary breathed in deeply, she loved the smell of the Everything. It was in a constant state of motion; the smell would shift and turn, but was always lovely. She closed her eyes and drew a deep breath. She smelled the deep wonderful smell again, and then, underneath it—

"NO!" Mary said, as she turned around. Teeny and Corb were suspended in mid-air and unconscious, caught in bronze clouds of the Void. Between them floated Mellie with a terrible grin on her face.

"How can you just stand there between all of these stinky plants?" she asked with a sneer, the scars on her face crinkling wickedly. "They are awful."

"What do you want?" Mary asked, desperate to keep the tremor of fear of out her voice.

"What do I want? What do I WANT?" Mellie laughed, high pitched and hysterical. "I want you, Murray Jangles, or whatever it is that they call you. I want you gone, out of the picture, finito, not here anymore."

"You're—you're—you're going to kill me?"

"KILL YOU? Cycles no. Why would I kill you? That would be messy. I need you gone, Mariah Jingle. I want to send you home. You know information that the pesky Resistors do not need to know. And as long as you are around, one of these days, you are going to give it to them. And then, where would we be? WHERE WOULD WE BE?"

"What do you mean?" Mary considered her options, as she cast around the garden at the golden plants near her. She needed something to help her rescue her friends. She reached out with her mind for WindRunner, but the connection was muffled and distant. She could hardly feel him. Mellie was not supposed to be here, she was supposed to be in the Imperial City.

"What do I mean?" Mellie asked, putting a finger to her lips in thought. "This substance, this silly Everything that I used to be a keeper of, is supposed to be so powerful. But do you know what's more powerful? Sadness, apathy, fear, and emptiness. We thought we would have to force People to give up their connection to the Everything, but it's been so easy. It's not hard to get you all to just stay in your houses, too afraid to leave home. Trapped in your own self-doubt and longing, with the thought that you are safe. The more we convince People to give up their right to live their lives, the stronger the Void grows. My master has concocted a plan so powerful, I will be a queen here and in the Shadowlands before we're through."

Mary looked down to find creeping tendrils of the Void snaking up her ankles and wrists. She felt dull, tired, and full of jealousy for Teeny and Corb. How could they just hang there like that? They were both supposed to be so powerful, but neither one of had foreseen this. Mary didn't even like it in LeeChee, she realized, as the Void swirled up around her middle, cloaking her lower body in a tight bronze mist. She could go home to where she was loved, cared for, and cherished. She began to focus on her living room and bedroom, feeling the want and need to be in her parent's house again. To leave this wild adventure behind.

As Mary felt more drawn back to her home, she cast a lazy glance around the garden, looking at the golden plants with disinterest. Gold was a silly color for anything. So obvious. She couldn't wait to get out of here.

Mellie ranged around the small circle of the garden, babbling to herself and laughing wildly. She reached out to the weeping willow Mary had curtsied to moments before and tried to grab a piece of the plant.

"This is what we need. This is what we need," the deranged woman muttered to herself. "Towns in Thrall is nice and all, but these plants, these plants will give us so much more power."

As Mellie reached out a hand to grab a branch of the tree, another one of the willow's limbs swung through the air and knocked the small woman across the circle of the garden. Mellie landed with a thump next to the fountain and struggled to sit up. Mary's mind cleared for a moment and she heard WindRunner clearly via their Mindspan.

You must focus, Mary Jingo. You must focus on the Everything. I am coming to you, but you must focus.

Mary looked down and saw that the bronze mist of the Void had receded from her middle section back down to her feet. She looked around at the beautiful plants and focused on all of the best things. The smells that had comforted her and supported her through this journey so far. She thought about her friends and family at home, how much she loved riding her bicycle, and how she loved to spend time lost in books. As Mary focused on the Everything, a blast of golden light erupted from her hands, as it had on her first night in LeeChee, dissolving the bronze mist that held Teeny and Corb. Her friends slumped to the paving stones and groaned, as they rubbed their faces. Mary ran to their side.

"What happened?" Corb asked, as she sat up.

"I feel like I just had the most terrible dream," Teeny said.

"We were attacked by Mellie," Mary said, realizing that Mellie was still nearby. She looked over at the small woman. She was knocked out cold on the paving stones.

"By the Cycles!" Corb exclaimed, as she saw Mellie laying nearby. "You stopped her?"

"I thought that she had attacked the Imperial City. That's why they all left—" Teeny said, standing up and wobbling on her feet. She walked over to Mellie and poked her with the toe of her sandal.

"I don't know what happened. I just focused on the Everything, and this is the result," Mary said. Corb and Teny looked at Mary with pride.

"We should bind her. We should take her to the tower. Lady Kathryn and Heavy Dill will know what to do," Corb said.

Teeny and Corb stood side by side and worked their hands in a series of complex gestures. They pushed the golden web they wove towards Mellie. It bound itself to the woman and held her in place.

WindRunner landed next to the fountain with a rush of wind, his talons gleaming and his beak sharp.

"We're okay, WindRunner," Mary said to the Thunderbird, running a hand down his beak.

"I have already informed Oracle Heavy Dill and Lady Kathryn of this attack. They have sent two of the Thunderbirds that had been left behind to collect the prisoner. They want the three of you back in the tower immediately."

Mary nodded, and looked at Mellie lying unconscious on the ground. Her stomach turned slightly. Something about all of this gave Mary a sinking feeling. As two additional Thunderbirds circled overhead, Mary followed Teeny and Corb and climbed on WindRunner's back. WindRunner again jumped into the sky.

CHAPTER
FOURTEEN

Heavy Dill and Lady Kathryn asked Mary, Corb, and Teeny to go over the encounter with Mellie for the fourth time. They sat in the study on the sofa and chairs in front of the fire where the O.I.T.s had napped the day before. Heavy Dill paced in front of the fireplace. Mary had offered to show them the memory, but Lady Kathryn said that both her and Heavy Dill were much too exhausted to perform such a complicated bit of controlling.

"And she just appeared?" Lady Kathryn asked again.

"I don't really remember," Teeny told them again. "I was looking at the fountain in the garden and the next thing I knew, I felt half asleep, trapped in a terrible dream."

"It was the same for me," Corb said. "It all happened out of nowhere."

"I looked at the weeping willow and she appeared behind me," Mary added. "She said that she wanted to send me home. That I knew something that would help you all."

"This is all very troubling," Heavy Dill said, pausing with a hand on his chin. "I don't like holding her here. She is too powerful."

"We don't have a choice, Dill. Cody and the army are over a day's flight away. We have sent them messages, but they cannot return any faster."

"I say we raise the shields around the tower, with your permission, of course. I know that we five are really the only ones who are here overnight, but it seems necessary," Heavy Dill said. Lady Kathryn nodded in response.

"Where is everyone else? Don't they all live here?" Mary asked. She had seen so many People in the halls since she first arrived in Luminos.

"Most of our scholars, thinkers, and other People live in the City itself. Only oracles in Training live here full time. We used to have more students, but lately, I'm afraid more rooms than ever are gathering dust," Lady Kathryn said with a sigh. "I think it is time for the three of you to go to your rooms. You cannot help us more tonight."

"I don't know if I will be able to sleep," Teeny said. "That was all so scary."

"Why don't you all sleep in Mary Jingo's room?" Kathryn suggested. "Since it's technically guest quarters, the room should be able to provide beds for all three of you."

The three O.I.T.s told Lady Kathryn and Heavy Dill goodnight and went back to Mary's room. They hardly spoke to each other on the way. They shared a common silence of not knowing what to say.

When they walked into Mary's room, Corb said, "Two more beds for guests, please!"

Golden mist swirled in the air and two comfortable cots appeared. The three of them agreed that they would all like to get some sleep. Minutes after they laid down, Mary could hear Teeny snoring. She laid awake, staring at the ceiling, thinking about the mirror she had used to contact her parents and wondering when she would be able to use it again.

Mary jolted from sleep deep in the night hours as something exploded outside the window. She heard a scream and a shout, as a bright light flashed through the panes of glass. She ran to the window and looked out to see the courtyard below her on fire. Her stomach dropped to her feet. Bronze explosions bounced off a golden shield around the tower. They rocked against it and sprayed fire and sparks as the explosions could not get through.

She scrambled back to the bed and grabbed her golden goggles. She placed them over her eyes.

Any one there? she called, searching the inside of her mind for anyone's presence.

I'm here, Mary, she heard Heavy Dill's voice say.

What's going on?

I don't know. I think we're being attacked. The three of you need to stay where you are. The wards on your room will hold.

An explosion sounded outside of Mary's window so forcefully that the building rocked around her. She momentarily lost focus in her conversation. Corb and Teeny ran to the window, both shouting. Mary felt WindRunner at the corner of her mind, beating on the door to be let inside.

Mary! Mary! Are you still there? Heavy Dill said urgently.

Yes! We're okay. We're here.

Good. Stay where you are. I, or Lady Kathryn, or WindRunner will come to find you once we know what's going on.

Okay.

Mary felt the connection end. Another explosion rocketed so close to Mary's window, that she was blinded by a brilliant flash of bronze light. WindRunner's presence was nearby. Mary knew that he was trying to find her amid the chaos outside her window. She focused through the goggles on their bond.

Mary? Mary? By the Cycles, are you all right? He cawed over the Mindspan.

Yes, WindRunner! We are all right. Heavy Dill says to stay where we are.

I think that is wise. I can't get to you, Mary. The shield is too strong. I cannot fly through it. Your chamber is warded and safe for now. I would not ask you to leave.

What's happening out there?

A small group of Shoeboxians have attacked the City. They are searching for Mellie. My brothers in arms that stayed behind and I are trying to find them all, but they are moving too swiftly. Something evil has made it so that we can hardly see them.

Okay. We'll stay where we are.

She turned back to Corb and Teeny. They both stood next to their cots, eyes wide.

"Did you talk to Heavy Dill? WindRunner?" Corb asked.

"Yes. They want us to stay here. Heavy Dill says that the wards will hold," Mary replied.

"I don't like this one bit," Teeny said, nervously rocking from foot to foot.

"Heavy Dill said that they would come get us when it was safe. I think we should just stay here for now," Mary said.

Mary looked around the room. She needed something to take with her, just in case. Something that they would be able to take on a journey. The walls of the room glowed gold briefly and a black backpack appeared in the center of the floor.

"What's that for?" Corb asked. "We're supposed to stay here."

"Thank you," Mary said to the walls, as she slung the backpack over her shoulders. She checked to make sure the dissipator was in her pocket. "I don't know. They said they would come get us, it just seemed like we might need it."

"Well, I for one, think everything will be fine," Corb said. "Heavy Dill is very wise and he would not tell us to stay put——"

The walls around them shook with a force so strong, that the glass in the windows cracked, splintered, shattered, and exploded. Mary threw her hands up in front of her face, as her goggles flew off her head. She closed her eyes, as she was thrown across the room by the blast. A heavy, awful scent filled her nose.

Corb threw a shield at the glass, as Teeny used the Everything to slow Mary's fall to the floor. Teeny then ran to Mary, grabbed her by the arm and pulled her towards the trapdoor. As they made the top step, a giant, nasty Shoeboxian bared its teeth and snarled at them as it landed through the broken window. Corb screamed and ran after them. They crashed onto the ladder and Corb slammed the door shut above them. Teeny ran her glowing hand around the edge of it.

"I sealed it," she said breathlessly, as they came to the bottom of the stairs and into the hallway. "I don't know how long it will hold."

"What was that thing," Corb said, fear in her voice.

"That's a Shoeboxian," Mary said, the stink of it still in her nostrils.

"How did it break the shield?" Corb said, as they ran down the hall. "That shield was crafted and reinforced by every oracle and forecaster who has ever walked these halls. They shouldn't be able to break through."

"This isn't the time for a history lesson, Corb. We have to get to the study," Teeny said. The hallway around them rocked and lurched as explosions continued to pepper the shield.

Are you okay, Mary Jingo? WindRunner called, his voice full of worry. *I will break through this shield if I have to.*

I am! We made it out, WindRunner. The Shoeboxians, one of them got through. We're going back to the study.

They are through the shield? Be ready, I will find a way to fly to you.

Okay, Mary said.

"Where is WindRunner?" Teeny asked aloud. "I swear I felt his presence just now."

"He can't get through the shield," Mary replied, breathlessly. If she remembered correctly, they should be close to the study. "He is coming to find us."

Mary, Corb, and Teeny rounded a final bend and were in front of the door to the study. Corb threw it open, and Teeny stayed behind to seal it as Mary and Corb ran down the stairs into the room.

"Now what?" Teeny asked, as she joined them in the middle of the room. Teeny's pants and shirt were covered in dust and dirt from the explosion. The study seemed more solid. The blasts outside the window felt further away.

"I guess we wait for Heavy Dill or Lady Kathryn or WindRunner to find us," Corb said, shrugging her shoulders.

"So, we just make tea and play games until someone comes to look for us?" Teeny said.

"What else should we do? We don't have any goggles. We can't contact anyone," Corb snapped. "We can't go out there, the courtyard is on fire."

The room around them rocked with force.

"What was that?" Mary asked slowly. She felt WindRunner's presence on her mind again.

MARY! MARY! Open the window! The tower is exploding from the inside. It is going to fall. You must jump. I can catch all three of you.

"OPEN THE WINDOW," Mary screamed. Corb raced across the room, the floor beneath them lurched and began to cave in. Teeny was hot on her heels. Mary looked over at the table with the mirror on it, as the floor began to crack beneath her feet. She pulled the dissipator out of her pocket and pointed it at the table. She pressed the small button on its side and in a flash of golden light, the table, the mirror, and several other stacks of books and instruments were sucked up into the dissipator. Mary shoved the device back into her pocket and ran towards Corb and Teeny who wrestled the window open. It slammed back with force, as the floor began to cave in.

"JUMP!" Mary yelled, as she ran past Teeny and Corb. She didn't have time to think, as she put her foot on the ledge and launched herself into the night sky. She landed with a hefty thud on WindRunner's armored back. Teeny landed next and rolled out of the way as Corb landed behind her.

Hold on! WindRunner called to the three of them via Mindspan. The golden shield around the tower was a memory, as a soft golden haze sparkled in the air. The tower behind them began to crumble, as explosions continued up the inside of the building. As WindRunner sped away, the left tower of Luminos fell.

WindRunner shot through the sky, so fast that Mary closed her eyes. He sped away from the crumbling rock, dust, and glass. Explosions sounded around them.

Where do we go, WindRunner? Mary asked frantically. In front of them, a bronze-mist began to swirl and take shape. WindRunner slowed down, so not to fly through it.

"Oh no," Mary said aloud.

"What is that?" Teeny asked, fear in her voice.

The mist began to swirl and take shape. It whirled around, and formed Mellie's face in mid-air, the mist rippling as she smiled nastily, the scars on her face alive and whirling in the dark night sky.

"You thought you could get away that easily?" Mellie's voice was amplified and stretched. It was so loud that it blew Mary back. She clung to the handholds on WindRunner's back. "You can't get away from the Void, Mitzy Jingles. And you certainly cannot get away from me. It knows your name, it's seen your face. It hates YOU most of all."

"Stay away from us!" Mary shouted back at the Void.

"NO!" Mellie's face spat and laughed. "No, I will not. We got most of what we came for, your sweet Lady Kathryn and that other oracle to boot. I tried to leave you out of this, Shadowlands girl, but you just wouldn't LEAVE. So, now I'm going to have to, um, borrow your two friends here. The small curly-headed one seems like she will be especially powerful at helping me bend the Everything into the Void."

"We would never help you!" Teeny yelled from over Mary's shoulder.

"Oh, that is SO sweet," Mellie's floating face replied. "Unfortunately, you won't have a choice."

Mellie opened her mouth and bronze mist streamed toward them in a giant wave.

"WINDRUNNER! GET US OUT OF HERE!" Mary screamed.

"I cannot," WindRunner said, his wings barely flapping, as the mist began to swirl around them. "I am nothing, I think. I am not fit to be the Lumon's son. I can see it so clearly now."

Mary looked around, the mist swirled around them in great billowing clouds. What was she even doing here? Her family was so far away and she was not cut out for this. If only she could steal a Flike and take it home to show the other kids that she was cool. Then, then she would just be so happy!

Mary swayed in the cloud of mist, thinking of home. She could almost smell her neighborhood—the green scent of the grass and the tang of gentle salt on the air. She was so close to it. She just needed to focus and she could go home and be the coolest person in her class. They would never ignore her again.

Bright flashes of golden light flashed around Mary, but she was so close to her home, she didn't care. She felt her grip relax on the hand holds, and just as she was about to let go, a shower of golden sparks exploded next to them. Mellie's voice bellowed in rage, as a flying pirate ship floated into the mist. Cannons blasted golden Everything bombs from all sides, causing the mist to dissipate and recoil. Mary snapped back to herself, the thoughts of her neighborhood dissolving instantly.

"Are those...?" Teeny asked.

"Rough Riders," Corb replied.

The cannons continued to fire on the cloud of mist, as it shrunk from the golden spray of sparks.

WindRunner shook out his wings and cawed mightily, sending a jet of golden light from his beak, arcing towards the Void.

Hold on! he shouted to all three of them via Mindspan. He flew over the bow of the ship. He circled the vessel, once and then twice, as the crew waved a white flag over the rail. He came to a soft landing on the hard wood of the deck.

"Welcome aboard, Mary Jingo of the Shadowlands," said a tall, curvy woman with wild brown hair. "My name is McKeen and I'm the captain of this ship. We're here to bring you to safety."

Mary climbed down from WindRunner's back, putting her feet solidly on the wood planks of the deck. She turned and looked back to see the remaining two Towers of Luminos in the distance, ringed by fire, and the City's blue walls still glowing softly against the night sky.

AFTER

Mary watched Loey Cody walk through the rubble of the left tower of Luminos. He looked around at the piles of white rock and dust scattered around him.

"And Mellie told you that she took her?" he asked Mary for the third time.

"Yes," Mary said quietly. "She told us that she took both Lady Kathryn and Heavy Dill."

"How could I be so stupid?" Cody said, as he kicked a rock with the toe of his shoe across the pile.

"We were all deceived," Bonnie Judde said quietly. He stood to Mary's right, holding his hands crossed in front of him. "We will find them, Cody. We have to."

"Tell me what she said again," Cody said, turning and looking Mary in the eyes. "I need to hear it all again."

"Um, she threatened to send me home. She said—," Mary stopped speaking as Bonnie Judde laid his hand on her shoulder.

"She's told us enough times, Cody," Judde said quietly. "Mary Jingo, we appreciate your help with this. We have known for a long time that the Void existed, and that Mellie intended to use it. We just did not realize that it would be so soon."

"Is that how she got through the shield?" Mary asked. "By using the Void?"

"We believe so. The Void is the Everything turned inside out, so we think the Shoeboxians were able to use enough of it to slice through the shield. That, or Mellie did it from inside the tower. We do not know for certain."

Cody walked back toward them. Mary smelled something sharp from him, a smell of regret and remorse.

"What's done is done," Cody said. "If only we had the Mirror, we might be able to get a hint of where they were taken."

"Um," Mary said, her stomach tightening. "I may be able to help with that."

"What?" Bonnie Judde said, looking at Mary with shock.

"Well, I found a dissipator in the study the other night and I grabbed it, because I didn't know if I would need it."

"You stole it?" Loey Cody said, folding his arms across his chest.

"I borrowed it," Mary continued. "I used it to take the mirror, because I wanted to be able to see my parents again."

Loey threw his head back and laughed. Mary grinned in spite of herself.

"You are full of surprises, Mary Jingo. This is the best news I have heard all day. WindRunner called you warrior. I think you have earned the title."

"So," Mary said, quietly. "You are not going to send me home?"

Loey Cody looked at Bonnie Judde and then back at Mary.

"Will you stop asking me that?" he said with a smile on his face. "Why would we send you home? Mellie very clearly thinks that you know something that we need to know," Loey Cody said. "You and Van Clare and Teeny and Corb leave for Festdelm tomorrow to begin training again."

Mary's eyes lit up.

"Really?!" she exclaimed.

"Yes," Loey Cody said. "But next time you would like to have something, please ask. We are always happy to share."

He gave her a quick wink, and strode away from the rubble of the tower, toward the gate facing the mountains.

ACKNOWLEDGEMENTS

This book has taken too long to write with so many people's dedicated help, that I don't even know where to begin. If I had not ended up in China ten years ago, teaching English, I have no idea if this book would have been written. First and foremost, I would like to thank Cindy Conger, who read Mary Jingo's first story, which was a 110,000-word jumble of thoughts, phrases, and scenes lifted directly from *Game of Thrones*, and said, "I think this is really something." Her tireless encouragement has spanned years of hard work and multiple versions of this story. In addition to Cindy, I would like to thank Courtney Guadagno, who used her master's degree in editing to help me get Mary Jingo off the ground, and also slogged her way through the most complicated version of this tale. To my loyal brothers, David and Daniel, who are experts in the fantasy genre and sat with me in dingy brunch spots and gave me copious notes about how to expand the depth and breadth of LeeChee. To Caroline Zavakos, who pursued agents for me when Mary Jingo was new and just out of the attic, and has offered more help than I probably deserved. To Grace Rock, Patrick Chappell, and Jada McNeill for offering advice when I needed it the most. And to my dearest nephews, Mace and Trig, who were my first pilot readers and best buddies. Their feedback about the way kids actually interact with technology in our modern age has been ineffable in its value. And lastly, to my partner-in-crime, dearest love, and forever best friend, Brian, for sitting on the couch and listening to me read all parts of *City of Lights* out loud. For designing the beautiful, one-of-a-kind cover to this book, and for delivering fizzy waters and coffee to me on weekend mornings when I needed to get edits done.

Kelly Byrd would like for you to know that she is very sorry about this. Stories have crept around the halls of her mind since she was a little girl. Not even the combined will of her two loyal pups, her devoted husband, and all of her house plants could keep her from putting this story into the world. (They would like you to know that they would have NEVER tried to stop her.) If you're ever in Nashville, Tennessee, please stop by Frothy Monkey East and tell her hello. She'll be the blonde woman on a laptop, pretending to write, while sipping an iced soy latte.

Made in the USA
Columbia, SC
30 May 2021

38331977R00174